Tales Out of School

Tales Out of School
Joseph Alengo

Rutledge Books, Inc.  Danbury, CT

Copyright © 2002 by Joseph Alengo

ALL RIGHTS RESERVED
Rutledge Books, Inc.
107 Mill Plain Road, Danbury, CT 06811
1-800-278-8533
www.rutledgebooks.com

Manufactured in the United States of America

Cataloging in Publication Data
Alengo, Joseph
  Tales Out of School

  ISBN: 1-58244-194-4

  1. Memoirs

Library of Congress Control Number: 2002094602

Introduction

    The title suggests that this entire narrative will be about school. Although much of it is connected in some way to school, some of it falls outside those parameters. In either case, it's been interesting, exciting, hilarious, outrageous, frustrating, happy, and miserable—yes, all of this and sometimes more.

    I've noticed over the years that I've been able to amuse, interest, and occasionally outrage friends and acquaintances with some of the subject matter contained in the pages which follow. It finally occurred to me that since most of these people have listened with more than merely courteous attention, perhaps a collection of observations, truths, opinions, and anecdotes would be of considerable interest "out there."

    I found after I got into the text that my memory seemed to be playing tricks on me. Maybe it's just that I'm getting older, but at times it didn't seem clear to me whether an experience about which I was writing had really happened, or whether I had spent some time at some point thinking the experience would be interesting. The lines of reality and unreality are sometimes blurred. Armed with faith that I have been honest in the past and will likely remain so throughout my lifetime, I plunged in.

Bad News Waller

We wanted Waller badly. As we saw it, they were one of the basketball teams in the north section capable of derailing our drive to the top. We were Schurz High School, located on Chicago's northwest side, usually one of the city's football powers, and not as often, basketball powers. It was January 1951.

"We've got to practice hard. We have to crash the boards," said my friend Raffe, our team leader, best scorer, and best player. He tended to be quiet but intense. We often imitated him good-naturedly: "How much time? What's the score?" He was quite nearsighted, and his refusal to wear glasses during a game didn't help.

"Don't let them get the ball to Jesse White if you can help it, and if it happens, do your best to make him give it up; and remember, we play defense with our feet. We have to move. Don't stand in one place and expect to get the job done," advised Dick Fee, our well-liked coach. White was the best player on Waller's team, a good scorer.

Max Saxinger, one of our smarter players, said, "Think before you move. Fake before you drive or pass. Keep 'em on their heels." In practice or in a game Max regularly did precisely what he advised others to do.

Frank Miller, a tough competitor, kept saying, "Don't let 'em push you around. You push them around. If they crowd you, jab 'em with an elbow." Frank did precisely what he advised others to do as well.

Caz Passalino was truly a role player. He couldn't shoot the ball into the ocean, but he could rebound well enough to help us. Now and then he'd take a shot if he was open, but after several misses decided not to take any but the easiest of shots. Often he went scoreless.

Waller was a slight favorite to win our section. They were good, and they were tough—I mean they were street-tough, too. Located in the inner city, in the same neighborhood as the infamous Cabrini-Green, the school was a reputed jungle with a student body which was intimidating to the point of being considered a "sixth man" on the floor when games were played there, which our game was. We were up for the challenge. We were cocky, and played a scrappy game. My teammates and I would do practically anything to win for dear old Schurz High. I remember my dad sneaking out of work early to see the game, played late on a Friday afternoon. His workplace was in Chicago's Loop area, within walking distance of our game. He didn't get to see me play much, and I was glad to spot him during pregame warmups.

"Boys," said Coach Fee during our pregame huddle, "just play your best and hardest. Don't worry about making mistakes. Play good defense. Remember, we play defense with our feet. Hustle, move. Don't stand around. Deny the pass to the inside, and try to keep the ball out of Jesse White's hands. Look for the fast break whenever we get a rebound or intercept a pass. Do your best, and the results will take care of themselves."

Play began, and the butterflies I was feeling went away in seconds. We got the ball first, and with the ball in my hands I immediately found myself open for a medium range jumper near the free throw line and made the first basket of the game.

"Way to go, Pal Joe," Frank said, slapping me on the back.

"That's the way to fire 'em," Max said, thrusting his fist in the air.

The bench erupted simultaneously, as if like we'd won the state championship instead of scoring only the first basket.

I felt a wonderful glow as I hurried back on defense. But Waller's Jesse White got down to the other end of the floor faster than any of us, and scored their first basket. Geez, I thought, I didn't even get any time to enjoy myself.

The game was very fast-paced from start to finish. It seemed that if you weren't alert every second, something bad would happen.

"Hoo, hoo, shoot! You could make it from here," I'd be saying to their outside shooters, trying to goad them into taking poor percentage shots. They instead tried to get the ball inside, but with only limited success, because my teammates were blocking off the passing lanes. Meanwhile, our leader Raffe picked up four baskets, Max took a couple of smart shots for scores, and Frank muscled in a couple. We found ourselves leading by three at the end of the first quarter.

"You're playing super basketball," said Coach Fee when we came to the bench.

"Hang in there. Take it to those SOBs," said my pal Jim Brahm, a hard-nosed substitute whose rough-and-tumble style helped kill some game time when a starter needed a breather.

"We can take these guys," yelled Fenny (whose real name was Don Fenton), who often came into a game to give me a rest. Fenny could be counted on to provide scoring. He had a good eye for the basket, and he wasn't afraid to shoot as some substitutes are.

"Is anybody tired?" asked Coach Fee. All voices denied the fatigue factor.

Midway through the second quarter, Raffe, after scoring yet another of his several baskets, ran back on defense very close to my ear. "How much time? What's the score?" he asked, as usual.

Though it doesn't seem to make any sense, these words comforted and inspired me.

After Max rebounded a missed Waller shot, I drove the lane and was fouled vigorously by Waller's Tony Perone.

"Let the clown drive. He can't hurt us," admonished a

Waller teammate to Tony. This was a kind of indirect verbal intimidation some players practiced and got away with. The officials usually kept things in control and didn't allow direct physical or verbal abuse, but by saying this to one's own teammate, the player was able to get the point across, and the officials winked at it.

A short time later while we were on defense, a deflected pass bounced to me near the edge of the free throw circle. There seemed to be no one in front of me. I began to dribble the length of the floor as fast as I could. I soon discovered Tony Perone and Jesse White of Waller on my left side, slightly left of center. I dumped a blind bounce pass to Raffe, who was a couple of steps behind me slightly to the right. He always seemed to be in the right place. I knew he'd be there. Tony and I were running shoulder to shoulder. He started to come around the front of me (Lord, he was fast!) to block Raffe. At the free-throw line, I gave him a shove with my left elbow. Because of the high speed with which we were running, he lost his feet and slid on his back and side past the baseline and into a wall some ten feet beyond. There was a mat on the wall to cushion players who ran into it when they were standing, but the lowest two feet did not afford protection. Tony crashed into the lower section of the wall while Raffe scored the basket. It clearly was a foul on me. Everyone in the place saw it except the two referees. The Waller fans were furious.

At his first opportunity, Coach Fee sent Fenny in for me and motioned me to sit next to him on the bench.

"Joe, we play hard, but we don't play dirty," he said softly to me. "We don't want to try to hurt anybody. We just want to try to win."

Tony stayed in the game. "I'm okay. You can't hurt steel," he said with a swagger, and the Waller fans cheered him.

Coach sent me back in after a few minutes, but the attitude of the fans toward me remained unchanged. They yelled, "Hey, number ten, you're gonna get yours after the game." During the times when the ball went out of bounds on the side of the court and it was awarded to our team, I was the player who always inbounded the ball. We had a few plays for this purpose, and each of us had certain designated paths to run to make it work. The bleachers at Waller came to the sideline of the court. There was no space provided for a player inbounding the ball. I found myself standing among the home team faithful who were pulling the hair on my legs and pinching me.

"You better say your prayers, number ten," I heard behind me.

"You're dead meat," someone else said.

"Drop dead," I said when the referee was out of earshot, and "Stick it up yours."

Waller won the game by three points. It could've gone either way. I apologized to Tony Perone, and he graciously accepted, but the Waller fans were still unhappy.

"Can we get a little help to our cars, maybe an escort?" Coach Fee asked of the Waller coach. But police were already on the scene, school officials having alerted them at the first sign of trouble. They did, indeed, escort us to the cars of my dad, Coach Fee, and a few of our fans who had come to the game.

Later, at home, my dad tried to make light of the situation, but I recognized that he was serious behind his attempted breeziness.

"You certainly make life interesting sometimes," he began with a smile, "but you could've hurt that Waller boy. You should play hard, but you shouldn't play dirty."

"That's what Coach Fee said to me after it happened," I said.

"I know. I spoke with him while you were in the shower. He's a good man."

A year later, I met Tony Perone when we both registered for the fall semester at Wright Junior College in Chicago. I spotted him first and approached him, offering him a smile and a handshake. As soon as he saw me, he broke into a grin, shook the hand I offered, and said, "You can't hurt steel." He was a tough competitor and had a good sense of humor as well. "If you need any help in English, I'll help you," he offered (we were in the same class), "and I'll be happy to give you a few tips about playing better basketball," he added, with a crooked smile.

During that same year I bumped into Jesse White at a Waller dance I attended with a Waller girl I dated for a time. We got to talking.

"I want to form a group of poor, underprivileged kids and do something with them to give them recognition and keep them from running the streets and getting into trouble," he said. "Something not too complicated, something relatively easy, like tumbling. You know, acrobatic things—like somersaults, rolls, twists, gymnastic things like that, but I'd train them to be really good at it. I think we can do it and travel around the country with it. I'll try to get businesses to sponsor and pay for our travel and expenses."

My date had mentioned to me that Jesse spoke of this quite frequently, and I recognized that he'd spent considerable time thinking about it. It seemed an enormously ambitious project to me, and I had doubts that he could pull it off, but a few years later the Jesse White Tumblers were seen quite regularly on television in and around the Chicago area. The last time I saw the Jesse White Tumblers was as part of a parade at President William Clinton's second-term inauguration. I think Jesse White is a fine human being.

In December of 1998, I phoned a cousin of mine who graduated with him and, curious about his whereabouts and activities, asked her if she knew what he was up to these days. "Didn't you know?" she asked. "He was elected Secretary of State for the state of Illinois last election day in November." Somehow I had known many years before, even when we were in high school, that he'd achieve great things.

I learned recently that my old, dear friend Raffe was named and inducted into the Chicago High School Basketball Hall of Fame. He deserved it. He was the best player we had, and he absolutely dominated during those years. He telephoned me and said, "You helped me get there, so I thought you'd like to know," which I thought was very kind and thoughtful.

Yes, I helped him: I screened for him so he'd get a good look at the basket, but he would MAKE the shot almost every time, whereas others might not. Many times when the ball was in my hands, I'd drive the lane, drawing a defender to me, then bounce a pass to him (and occasionally others) near the basket. That's why I came to be often called "Pal Joe," which you'll see here and there in the text of this writing, creating easy baskets for my teammates. Raffe had an uncanny sixth sense. He KNEW when I was going to perform this maneuver. He simply "had a nose for the ball."

It was a pleasure watching him in action. I felt lucky to be alive to watch him. I should have bought roses and a box of cigars for my mom and dad for having me when they did. Yes, he had help, but he made the most of the little help he received. Oftentimes he had to create his own movements, usually ending in a basket for our team. If we had been professionals, he'd be putting money in our pockets. One post-game question I asked of an opposing player in the showers:

"What would you have had to do to win today?"

"Shoot Raffe Simonian," he said. And that pretty well says it.

The Laughing Man

In grade school, I had a certain lack of control which sometimes got me into trouble. It was an inability to stop laughing at precisely those times when doing so would have been advantageous to me. A funny situation or joke I was enjoying was supposed to come to a halt when the teacher looked our way, inasmuch as it usually was a digression from the lesson at hand. Most of the others could stop laughing on cue, and transform their dispositions instantly into expressions of serious, sober, and deep concentration on the matter being discussed. I was not blessed with this valuable skill.

Jack Boeglan sat next to me, and would often look me in the eye and say with a serious expression, "Pardon me, Sir, but do you know your fly is open?" or to the girl sitting in front of him, same serious expression, he would say. "Miss, I'm taking a survey. What bra size do you wear?"

After experiencing numerous and embarrasing reprimands from Sister Fiat, our sixth grade teacher (Yes, it was a Catholic elementary school), I became angry, and I blamed Jack.

"I'm sorry," he'd say, "I'm really sorry." And I believe he was, but it happened again.

"Jack, if it happens one more time, I'm going to fight you after school."

It happened one more time, and word of a confrontation spread quickly, but quietly, throughout the room.

"I don't want to fight you," Jack whispered to me five minutes before the bell, but I felt something had to be done, and besides, the whole class knew about it. My honor was at stake. If I had been smarter, I would have skipped the fight, made up some excuse.

Jack and I duked it out at the corner nearest the school. It was a bitter cold January day, and several of the kids who had come to see the fight decided to go home where it was warm. Jack and I punched, rassled, and rolled around on some icy walks and decided, after a time, to end it from sheer exhaustion. We congratulated each other on a good fight, shook hands and were friends again.

"I promise I won't make you laugh again," said Jack.

"Hell, it's my fault. I need to control my laughing,"

Another time, Richard Radke sent me a note from across the room. There must have been seven or eight kids who passed the note along. Rich was a guy who'd say things like "I'm a stud, and all the girls are after me. Treat me right, and I'll give you a lesson or two."

I opened the note which said, "Smile if you've been making it with Marilyn S."

I not only smiled. I broke out into an absolute peal. Rich, who had been intently watching the note being passed and read, didn't realize that Sister Fiat was moving quickly toward him from behind. She whacked him on his back a moment before I burst out laughing, then moved quickly toward me, then stood before me, her arms crossed menacingly across her chest, outwardly angry, watching me laughing and out of control. Suddenly SHE burst out laughing as loud as I was, and at that moment, the entire class began laughing uproariously.

"Oh, Jesus, Mary, Joseph, help me," she yelled, as she went back to the front of the room, motioning with her arms toward heaven, still laughing. We liked her during moments like that.

FIRE

A few years later I was in high school. I tried out for, and somehow made, the basketball team. The first couple years I hardly played. I managed to get in for a short time near the end of a game if we were around 20 points ahead or behind. At the time we didn't have, as many high schools do today, a freshman team, a sophomore team, a junior varsity team and a varsity. We had a team. Period. Some years later there were two levels: Frosh/Soph and Varsity. In these situations, we were inclined to take some ill-advised shots and foul quite a bit. We weren't really that bad. There was another motive: In those days, oftentimes a full box score appeared in the Chicago newspapers. A player had to score or foul in order for his name to appear in the box score.

If I sound like I'm complaining, my friend George Feuerschwenger (pronounced fire schwinger) saw even less playing time for a while, owing to his long name, which was also most difficult to spell. (Take another look at it.)

"I hope we get in this game," George would say to me before the start of each one.

"Yeah, so do I," I'd reply. "We need the experience."

Eventually, our wish came true.

"You five guys go into the game," the coach said to us with barely two minutes remaining. "Don't forget to report to the scorer's table."

The first few times a group of us reported to the scorer's table as the preliminary to entering the game for our minute or so until its conclusion, the others of us with simple, easily spelled names entered the game, but poor George: The scorer would say, "Just a minute, Kid. Spell that for me," and he'd write

George's name in the official scorebook as it was spelled for him.

Meanwhile, the game had resumed, and by the time the scorekeeper finished with George's name—there were interruptions because of fouls, baskets scored, etc. which needed the scorekeeper's attention —the game was over, and George hadn't played. After this happened three times, George wised up. The next time at the scorer's table to enter the game, when asked his name, he said "Fire," and ran onto the court. That's how his name appeared in the box score. Not only was it a sensible shortening of his surname, but his bright red hair and his quick energetic movement strongly suggested that part of his destiny was to be called Fire. Many of the students, three years later at graduation time were astonished to see his name listed in the yearbook as George Feuerschwenger under his picture. They knew him as Fire.

NOT EXACTLY EXCITING, OR WAKE ME WHEN IT'S OVER

Many of my memories of high school are of basketball because frankly, I was, and still am, a basketball nut. I probably had no business making the team in the first place. I am not gifted with great size. I shot well, but not great; I ball-handled and passed well, but not exceptionally well. There probably were kids walking the halls who had better skills than I. But I had great desire and a willingness to work hard. In addition, I had a self-confidence which bordered on outrageous. I think now, years later, that the coach saw these qualities as being important enough to offset any skill deficiencies. I made the team as a sophomore, and eventually became a starter in my senior year. In the meantime, there was a lot of bench-warming and a lot of hard work in practice.

But there were moments. There was a game at Senn High School on the city's north side in January, 1949. I remember having made all my shots, and there were several, in pregame warmup. Other than a smile from the coach, this feat passed quietly. Near the end of this game, I was dozing at the far end of the bench opposite the coach. (He seated players he intended to use near him). I was a sophomore and hadn't played much. I felt an elbow jabbing me in the ribs; it was my friend and teammate Don Finn awakening me.

"Pal Joe, Coach is calling you. Gene Serzynski's fouled out."

I did my best to shake the cobwebs out of my head. When I huddled with the other players on the floor, they seemed to be excited and breathless. I remember Ray Domain, the captain, saying "Glad you're in, Pal Joe. You can help us. Just do your best and don't worry about making mistakes." He had a way of making you feel a part of things. He was a good player, and people liked him.

Then play resumed. I had no idea how much time was left or what the score was, although I never had played unless we were approximately twenty points ahead or behind near the end of a game. Almost immediately Fire (star of the previous story), who was getting more playing time now, being pressured in the backcourt, threw an errant pass which hit a referee, and was headed out of bounds in the upcourt left corner, away from everyone, but from my position on the left side, I chased it, and wondered why the audience seemed so excited. I reached it before it went out of bounds, and the noise level intensified to a point, it seemed to me, where someone might think of measuring it in terms of the Richter Scale.

"Put it up, Pal Joe," screamed Don Finn.

"Shoot, Joe, You're hot," shouted Coach Fee.

"Your shoelace is untied," I heard a Senn fan yell, trying to divert my concentration.

No one else was around me. I was in the deep corner behind the backboard, where a shot attempt would have to arch above the board, something you attempt for laughs, maybe, if you're with some friends in an otherwise empty gym in a non-game situation.

But I had much success shooting in the pre-game warmup, so I thought, "What the hell, why not?" I let go a 22 footer which hit the back of the rim (from the direction I shot), bounced straight up, and dropped through the hoop for 2 points (This was before the 3-point shot). An even louder roar exploded from our supporting fans which startled me, and when I glanced up at the scoreboard, I was surprised to see we were one point ahead with less than a minute to play.

I hadn't realized the game was so close. Now I was frightened, thinking about my crazy shot. I wonder if I'd have made it if I had realized the gravity of the situation.

"Great shot, P.J."."Way to go, Pal Joe," came happy comments shouted from teammates on the bench. "I knew Coach sent in the right man," said Ray to me, slapping me on the back.

Senn immediately called a timeout. When we huddled with our coach, he advised,

"Don't let them get the ball inside. Play a tight zone nearer the basket. Don't let them drive to the basket. Make them beat us with an outside shot. Let's take our chances with that."

We went into a tight zone, as ordered. We cut off the passing lanes. The Senn players passed the ball around the perimeter for a few seconds.

"Deefense, deefense," our small group of fans yelled.

Senn used a few more seconds, deliberately passing the ball around the perimeter. Then Leon Rane, their scrappy little guard, drove the lane, missed the shot, but the ref called a foul on Ray. Rane was a good competitor, and moves such as this had become a trademark of his—so much so that "Rane Drives the Lane" became almost a household phrase on Chicago's north side for a couple of years. My new status as hero was tarnished somewhat when he made both free throws and won the game for them.

WHO'S ON FIRST?

I remember playing at Sullivan High School, also on Chicago's north side, later in January that same year, and both teams showing up wearing gold jerseys. Gold were our away jerseys; white were our home jerseys. Sullivan must have had a poor athletic fund. Gold jerseys were their home AND away uniforms. Sullivan's coach had called our coach, and they agreed a week previously that we would suit up in our white jerseys, but our coach forgot to tell us. It would be impossible for the officials to officiate, and so the Sullivan team played in their white undershirts with numbers having been written hastily with magic markers. We won the game, but it was of no consequence because neither team was going anywhere that year.

After the game in the locker room, two of our guys, a couple of screwball underclassmen substitutes we all liked because of their energy and outrageous sense of humor, were involved in some towel-snapping type horseplay. They were Gene Franklin and Buckey Singer. Coach was still upstairs. One of them ran toward a closed door, pushed it open as he hurried through it, and we heard a splash. We immediately heard a second splash as his pursuer streaked through the doorway.

"Hey, you guys," they yelled.

Three of us went through the doorway in the direction of their voices, thinking they might be in trouble and need help.

"Come on in. The water's fine," they yelled, when we appeared on the other side of the door. They had fallen into the school's swimming pool. It seemed a good idea, so the whole team stripped down to the altogether and jumped in. We swam for approximately ten minutes, showered and dressed; Coach was none the wiser.

"Thanks for finding us a new swimming hole," Ray said to them afterward. "Yeah, good show," said Max, and the other guys expressed their gratitude as well. It lent itself to much comraderie.

The next school day word reached several of us to come to Ray's table at lunch. After we were gathered there, Ray said, "We are together today to honor Gene and Buckey who, in their diligent explorations, found for us a new swimming hole. I therefore present to them the Royal Order of Swimming Hole Explorers."

"Hear, hear," and "A toast to Gene and Buckey," and "A credit to mankind," etc. we found ourselves saying. Ray presented them with medals he and Max had fashioned out of tin from one of the shops and ribbon from the home economics department. We all applauded heartily.

"We shall wear these awards proudly the remainder of the day," said Gene and Buckey.

I felt a warm glow from this, and my teammates did as well. Maybe it was a coincidence, but we won our final three games of the season after that.

ORDER ME A HERO SANDWICH

During the course of my four years at Schurz, I met and became good friends with Roy Kolsky. He was a grade behind me, but lived fairly close to me, about a mile. We spent a lot of time playing sandlot type basketball at the YMCA as well as watching a lot of TV at one another's homes.

Rip (as he was called) was a superb football player (a wonderfully gifted, glue-fingered pass-catching end) and baseball pitcher, and represented Schurz in those sports.

We had great fun during the classes we had together. I recall our English teacher, Mrs. Elsa Schmidt, asking for volunteers to act out the Romeo and Juliet balcony scene. I volunteered for Romeo. It was exactly the reason old Mrs. Schmidt couldn't then get any girls to do the part of Juliet.

"Won't anyone do Juliet's part?" Mrs. Schmidt asked, obviously disappointed. (Several of the girls admitted later that, although they were ready to do Juliet, none of them was willing to risk it with me doing a burlesque of Romeo). So old Rip says, "I'll be Juliet."

Knowing this was her last hope, she allowed it. So Rip put a handkerchief around his head and tied it under his chin, looking surprisingly like a girl. Then, using a chair, climbed up on top of the closet (where teachers hang their coats).

"....Romeo, Romeo, wherefore art thou, Romeo?" Rip began, and in looking down at me, temporarily lost his footing and came perilously close to falling to the floor on his head. If this were a comedy, any critic would say it was a huge success, based on the laughter in the audience. Mrs. Schmidt laughed too; she was a good sport.

And so it went. It was a joy being with him. It appeared to me at the time, that this was the beginning of a lifelong friendship.

During a football game in the fall of my senior year, Rip got kicked behind the ear in a pileup, lapsed into unconsciousness, and, though still obviously breathing, could not be awakened. He was taken immediately to the hospital.

For a time, about two weeks, Rip was not allowed any visitors other than his parents. As soon as we were able, my dad and I went to visit him there. I was shocked by what I saw. Here was my pal, Rip, looking like a ghost, with tubes connected to his body here and there. He seemed to have lost an enormous amount of weight. Two weeks before, he was around 190, and now he looked like he perhaps didn't reach 100 pounds. And he was still asleep. They had not been able to awaken him.

"Rip, it's Pal Joe," I said. "How're ya doin?"

But he didn't respond. He seemed to be in another world.

"Come on, Rip, talk to me. What happened to my old buddy who's never at a loss for words? Talk to me, Rip."

No response. Then I suddenly realized Rip wasn't going to make it. He was going to die. Neither the doctor nor his parents mentioned his coming death, but I knew it.

I burst into tears. "You'd better not die on me, you son of a bitch." I was angry at him, angry at God, angry at the injustice of it all. "Please, please talk to me," I sobbed. This continued for a few more minutes, loudly enough for the nurses to become alarmed. Soon Rip's nurse came in and advised us to leave. I'll never forget that day as long as I live.

Three weeks later, Rip died. I felt alone.

Asked to give a eulogy in church at the funeral, I found that, even though I accepted the honor, I couldn't do it. I couldn't get past a couple of lines practicing it before breaking into a flood of tears. I also passed out during the part of the funeral at the gravesite. Trying mightily to hold back tears, I suddenly lost consciousness. I was revived almost immediately, having bloodied my nose and dirtied my face, but I didn't care.

I became a loner for a time. Many kids told me how sorry they were because I was one of Rip's best friends, but I barely saw them. I was in a funk. Sometimes during a class, I would start crying and have to walk out. Nothing seemed to be fun anymore. I was even seeing a psychiatrist for a time at school. He said that if I could come to terms about Rip's death, I could beat this depression, and perhaps forget him.

"But I don't want to forget him," I said. "What purpose would that serve? I know you're trying to help me, Doc, but forget it. I wish I was dead too."

But the psychiatrist stayed with me, refusing to give up on me, and it paid off. Somehow he got me to realize that life is worth living. This is not to say I don't remember Rip, but I came to look upon his memory as a gift.

Schurz High School initiated the Roy Kolsky award a year later, after I had graduated, to be given to an athlete of good character. The first of these awards went to Gerry Voelz, also a good friend, probably his best friend, and his catcher when he pitched in a baseball game representing Schurz.

Four years after I graduated from Schurz, and was attending Northern Illinois University, I wrote a short story about the Rip Kolsky experience for a creative writing class. I had recently won first place for another story in the school's annual literary magazine, but the professor's and the class' consensus was that the story about Rip was the better of the two. I thought so too.

OLYMPIC GOLD

Our sixth period lunch table at Schurz High School in February, 1951, was a motley mix of guys, many of them jocks. We had a couple of basketball players, four football players (two of them quite large interior linemen), a couple non-jocks and Terry McCann.

We were a rather loud, boisterous and breezy bunch who sincerely liked one another, but showed it by putting down each others' accomplishments:

"How'd you get away to score on that 23-yard touchdown run? You must've bribed those defenders." Or,

"P.J. got an 'A' from old lady Burke? Must have been a typographical error." And,

"How'd you manage to beat the defense down the floor for that basket just before halftime? You usually run like you've got a piano on your back."

It sounded like a Friar's Club roast. And we loved it. But the one guy who seemed to be a bit more serious than the rest of us was Terry. He was a wrestler, a very good one, a little guy who might otherwise look a bit out of place, especially alongside one of the interior football linemen. If wishing and admiration were inches, I'd have him a giant in no time. Things being what they are, though, he stood five foot six, no more than that. I'd say he weighed around 115, maybe 120. He was disciplined and focused, and we loved him, but how we chided him for it:

"How about some ice cream, Terry? I'm buying," one of us would say. Or,

"Want some of these french fries? They're really good today."

All requests were met with a smile and a quiet refusal. The most blatant attempts at persuading Terry came on Thursdays.

25

That was the day of the week when the lunchroom special was turkey with stuffing, mashed potatoes and a green vegetable for 35 cents. Even in 1951, it was a bargain. Most of us would go back to buy a second turkey lunch, and a couple of the football players even went back for a third.

"Terry, this is really good," and "You should really try it. You'd love it." And on and on.

But old Terry would simply smile and dig into his fruit salad. It helped him maintain his weight for wrestling purposes.

Terry was the state champ that year in his weight division. He then went to one of the Iowa colleges with a superb wrestling program, and before we all quite realized it, went to Rome in 1960 to compete in the Olympics. Yes, he won the gold medal in that Olympic competition and even appeared on television in a commercial touting Wheaties, Breakfast of Champions a year or so later.

But I think the crowning touch in all this was when I received a phone call from a close friend of Terry's a couple days after he won the gold medal.

"There's going to be a party day after tomorrow, this Saturday, at Terry's house."

"But isn't he still in Rome? They won't be back Saturday."

"Yeah, I know, but his mother is so excited, she wants to have one now, and then another later when he comes home."

So it came to be that a party was held with the guest of honor being absent.

FENNY'S INJURY

On a day when we had a game scheduled at Lane Tech, a few miles east of us on Addison Street, I was sitting in music class on the third floor at one end of the triangle, so named because the hall had that shape. Lane Tech had the highest enrollment in the city, and it was an all-boy school, so they usually had good athletic teams. It was eighth period, and after this class, we were usually given permission from our ninth period teacher to skip that class so we could be on time for the game in the late afternoon.

We took public transportation. Sometimes a team member was able to persuade his eighth period teacher to excuse him because some of the teachers didn't read their bulletins, and trusted the boys. Usually we were trustworthy, but occasionally one of us was not.

As I casually looked out from my seat near a window, I was amazed to see my friend and teammate Don Fenton mugging at me with crossed eyes and a grotesquely contorted face. He resembled a horror movie monster in an amusing way. He had been excused from his eighth period class, and decided to have some fun with us. He had climbed the fire escape. After a few other kids in class became distracted, and looked out the window, the teacher, Mrs. Edna Sweitzer, looked there too, but Fenny ducked out of sight.

This continued for several minutes, then stopped as suddenly as it had started. After class I learned that Fenny scratched his face near the corner of his eye on a rusty nail sticking out of the mortar between the bricks. It looked a bit nasty, but we reasoned that with a little cleaning and attention, he could play in the game.

At Lane when Coach saw Fenny's eye, he sent him to the nurse. He came back a short time later with his face and part of his head wrapped quite elaborately, it appeared.

"No basketball for me today, Coach," he said.

"What?" asked coach Dick Fee.

"Yeah, the doc said."

"A doctor?" asked coach Fee. "I can't believe it. This is incredible. It didn't seem like a serious injury to me," he said. "Come with me, Fenny. We need to see about this doctor."

When they investigated with the office, the assistant principal seemed to know immediately what the cause was. He took them to a corner of the locker room, and confronted what appeared to be a young man.

"Is this the doctor who treated you?" he asked Fenny. It was, but he wasn't a doctor. He was Wally Mulbury, a new player on Lane's team who looked older than he was, and liked practical jokes. He had been sitting in the nurse's office while the nurse was away from her desk taking a coffee break (There was no doctor). He completed the charade by wearing a white coat that doctors and nurses like to wear on the job.

They took off the elaborate bandages and fixed Fenny's eye with a little butterfly band-aid. He played.

Meanwhile, Wally Mulbury, the imposter, proved to be even more adept in his role as a basketball player. He played a great game, and beat us practically single-handedly, the louse.

HE WOULDN'T RAT ON THE BOYS

"What'll we do for excitement today?" asked Earl Strong. "It's so boring around here. We need a little adventure," he continued, with a mischievous smile.

"I'm sure you'll think of something," said Bill Hall.

"Come on, Earlie, think of something, encouraged Frank Kubon, Earl's close friend whose words of encouragement (or deviltry?) usually motivated Earl quite successfully, not that Earl often needed encouragement. The others of us agreed.

"Yeah, things are really dead around here," I said. The others nodded their yeses. It was lunch time at Schurz High School. After finishing lunch, the rules stated, students could stay in the lunchroom or they could go outside on the campus.

"All we can do is stay here or go outside," complained Earl. "I'm tired of it." He was a big, happy, popular kid, .a half grade level higher than I was, and a fine basketball player whose goal in life was to get as much enjoyment out of every minute of every day as he could. His energy level was ten times that of most kids. "Why can't we walk around the halls just for a little something different?" he asked. "Yeah, why not?" he answered himself.

"What've you got in mind?" I asked.

"I don't know. Let's go, and we'll think of something," he said.

It sounded reasonable to the rest of us not-so-deep thinkers, and we left the lunchroom to roam the halls.

After waving and mugging at kids we knew in classes as we walked by, peerless leader Earl shared his idea of a new adventure he thought of at that moment.

"Let's form a human pyramid and unscrew a fishbowl. We won't break it. We'll just unscrew it and put it on the floor in the corner." He was talking about the decorative covering used to cover the lightbulb, a typical idea from Earl who had been recently written up as a feature story on the sports page of the school newspaper with the opening line: "The kid with the crew cut, jokes and jump shots is Earl Strong."

"Yeah, great," said Bill. "I'll be on top and unscrew it." Bill was a popular kid too—one of the boys. The thing that distinguished Bill from everyone else was that he was the only black boy in the school at the time, winter of 1950. Plus the fact that he was a marvelously gifted athlete: a swift running back who could break up any football game with a big play (which he often did), and the anchor man on the conference winning track relay team. He was also very kind to people, had a wonderful sense of humor, and usually behaved himself.

We formed our pyramid, and Bill began unscrewing the fishbowl. We were in the triangle. It was a long hall in a large school. Suddenly Frank, in the middle of the pyramid said excitedly,

"Hey, you guys, there's Charlie Buehl!"

Sure enough, Mr. Charles Buehl, assistant principal and chief "hatchet man," of whom it was said ate students for snacks, came walking around the corner at the far end of the triangle. It was impossible to recognize his facial features from that distance, but he had a gait that was singularly his. The pyramid collapsed, and poor Bill ended up on the seat of his pants momentarily, but we all scrambled away before ol Charlie Buehl could get to us. He was too far away to recognize any faces, but, of course, Bill wound up in the office under interrogation by Mr. Buehl soon thereafter. But ol Bill didn't squeal on us, even though it was obvious that there were several boys in on the escapade.

"Why would a nice kid like you be walking the hall and doing a fool thing like that, Bill?" asked Mr. Buehl. "You're a good student, you get good grades, your teachers like you, you're a fine football player, and the kids look up to you. You're a leader; you need to set a good example."

"Bill, who were the other boys?" asked Mr. Buehl.

"You can do anything you want to me, Mr. Buehl," Bill said. "I'm not gonna rat on the boys. I ain't talkin." (Bill could be quite dramatic at times.).

"Bill, be reasonable. No one's going to jail, but everyone involved should be accountable."

"No, I'm not talking," Bill insisted.

Would Mr. Buehl conduct one of his now infamous Gestapo-type investigations (It was rumored around school that Mr. Buehl was a tough investigator and "always got his man.")? He decided to forego the investigation.

Bill was awarded two "encores" (so named for penalty periods served after school). It's obvious to me that Mr. Buehl liked Bill and secretly admired him for not ratting on us. A day later we were at our lunch table again, talking about it, laughing and joking.

"Yeah, ol Charlie Buehl spotted me right away because I'm shorter than the rest of you guys," Bill said.

What a guy, I thought. I could've thumped him on the back, I was so proud to be his friend.

Jesse Owens and the Lettermen's Club

Fridays at Schurz High School were club days. There were clubs for just about anything you can think of: cameras, Spanish, rods and guns, etc. A thirty-five minute period was squeezed between second and third periods, and all of the regular forty-minute periods were shortened by five minutes so that the school day would end at the usual time.

One Friday the Lettermen's Club had former Olympic track star Jesse Owens as our guest. He spoke to us about the value of education, working hard, and doing your best.

We were thrilled to have him there, talking to us, a group of about forty. I particularly remember one story he shared with us. Owens said that as a senior in high school, his high-school coach and he were going to board a train to a town in Ohio where the high-school basketball championship finals were taking place over a time span of three days.

Owens was on the telephone when his coach arrived at his house to pick him up. They were going to use public transportation to get to the train station. Owens, however, spent quite a bit of time on the phone, and it became clear that they were unlikely to get to the train station on time, so Owens's father drove them there, driving at times dangerously fast.

They ran when they were dropped off at the station and breathlessly asked a conductor, "Which train goes to the high-school basketball finals?"

"Track four. Hurry, or you'll miss it; it's leaving now." They scrambled to the train, hopping aboard as the train was leaving the station.

"Once on board and seated," Owens told us, "we observed

what we immediately concluded was peculiar behavior from the other passengers occupying this car on the train. After another ten minutes, we were certain these passengers were not in their right minds. We guessed these people were institutionalized. We tried to get out of this car, but there was no getting out from the inside.

"By this time Coach was so frantic, he resembled the other passengers. A few moments later, a young man in a white coat came in the door with a clipboard; he appeared to be counting heads and taking attendance.

"One, two, three. . . ." When he saw Coach, he asked, 'Who are you?'

"I'm Jerry Sullivan. I coach track and basketball."

"Oh, I see," said the young man, who appeared to be accustomed to answers such as these from these particular passengers. Unperturbed, he resumed his task. 'Four, five, six, seven. . . .'

"I felt bad about this, because my staying on the phone at home was probably responsible for this mess," Owens continued.

"'Please,' Coach said. 'There's been a terrible mistake. I coach track and basketball,' he said frantically, bolting from his seat toward the attendant.

"'Now you just sit there like a good little basketball coach,' the attendant said soothingly, guiding him back to his seat.

"'No, no, you don't understand,' Coach said.

"With that, the attendant left. About twenty minutes later, just when it seemed Coach and I were resigned to spending the rest of our lives in a mental institution, the attendant returned with a supervisor.

"Yes, we had unknowingly entered a car with institutionalized people, but it turned out we were on the right train after all. We moved into another car, and later enjoyed the basketball finals.

"And that just goes to prove the old adage," Owens concluded, "that getting there is half the fun."

YMCA

The YMCA had a program during those years for high-school-age boys, and it was good.

There was a Halloween dance coming up, and Mr. John Callahan, our sponsor, asked me to head a decoration committee and choose a couple of members to help me get the job done, and told me he would reimburse me for the expenses.

I chose John McClenden and Earl Spengler for my committee. Earl had use of a neat little pickup truck, and he also told us that an uncle of his had a farm just past the outskirts of the city. We could get all the cornstalks, hay bales, and pumpkins our hearts desired, for free. We would estimate their cost, tell Mr. Callahan, and he would reimburse us. Then we could have a party of our own in the near future.

On Halloween night the YMCA gym looked very appropriately alive, transformed with cornstalks, hay bales, pumpkins, ghosts, goblins, skeletons, and several rolls of black and orange crepe paper twisting overhead. In addition, we had borrowed some lights from the drama department at the high school and played them expertly upon the scene below, creating the spooky, eerie result for which we had hoped. The only things we paid for was orange and black crepe paper, skeletons, and ghosts and goblins.

"What a fine job you boys did," Mr. Callahan said to us. "It's decorated as fine as I've ever seen it. I can't get over how inexpensively you did the job. I'll reimburse you right after the dance."

The three of us looked at each other as if on cue, and became curiously quiet.

"I see I've embarrassed you with my compliments," he said

mistakenly. Then he left us to greet some of the others at the dance. Actually, we were embarrassed because we had underestimated the decorations cost by a longshot — and we were ashamed, too.

I looked at John and Earl. "We can't do this to Mr. Callahan," I said. They agreed. "No, we can't. He's a good guy," John said. "What made us think we should do it?" he asked, shaking his head. "What about you, Earl?"

"I feel awful; we can't do this," he said.

We quickly sought out Mr. Callahan, found him, and confessed. "Mr. Callahan," I said, "we can't do this to you."

"What's that?" he asked.

"We got almost all the stuff for the decorations free . . . ."

"Yeah," Earl said. "We got them all free from my uncle who has a farm just outside the city's northwest boundary."

"Yeah," John said. "Keep the money in the treasury. We would feel much better about it if you did that."

Mr. Callahan was quiet for a few seconds. Then he smiled a small smile and said, "I'm very proud of you boys. That's what this organization is all about—doing the right thing. I'm sure you boys feel good about it too."

We did. After the dance later that night the three of us sat around the dining room table at my house. I poured a glass of beer for each of us.

"Here's to Mr. Callahan and to honesty everywhere," I toasted.

"I'll drink to that," said John.

"Hear, hear," said Earl, raising his glass.

That's all we had to drink, one beer each. The rest of the evening was spent in relaxed conversation. We felt good about ourselves. I slept well that night.

To be perfectly honest about it, we felt as if a big weight had been lifted from our shoulders.

Baby, It's Cold Outside

Bud Walker, a good friend, came to me one day and said enthusiastically, "We should be in the variety show the school is putting on. We'll be a smash."

What he had in mind was to sing "Baby, It's Cold Outside," much like Johnny Mercer and Margaret Whiting had done some months before. I was to take the part of the girl.

I got the clothes and a suitable wig from a cousin of mine. She also did my makeup, and she was good. I really looked like a girl. With a little practice, I sounded like a girl, too. The emcee introduced us as Bud Walker and "Joanne" Alengo. Of course, the school kids knew me, and merely laughed aside the notion of "Joanne." We had a lot of fun doing it, and received much applause from the student body audience.

Mr. Fred O'Keefe, the football coach and sponsor of the Lettermen's Club, called me into his office a day or two later, and he told me we had been good and that several members of the Lettermen's Club had advised him to book us for an upcoming club variety show which was to be held after school hours. Admission would be charged, and it always was a well attended annual affair. Bud and I were flattered, and agreed to do it. Two former Schurz football stars, Johnny Miller and Don Stonsifer, were the emcees. They had both played for Northwestern in the 1949 Rose Bowl a year before, and were well known. Stonsifer was named to most All-America teams. They did a masterful job as emcees, and our act was very well received by the audience.

Then a strange thing happened. Johnny Miller, a good-looking young man who wasn't exactly afraid of girls, approached me backstage.

"Hi Joanne," he said. "I really enjoyed your act."

"Thanks," I said, smiling contentedly.

"Could I interest you in seeing the campus at Northwestern Saturday? I can pick you up, and we can make a day of it. I think you're one of the cutest girls around."

He thought I was a girl. It had not occurred to me that he might not know.

"Well, I, I don't kno-know," I stammered.

"Aw, don't be nervous," he said. "You'll love it."

He gave me his most dazzling smile, and I could see why girls might easily warm up to him.

"Whaddaya say? I'll be a good boy, and you'll love a look at college life," he said.

Bud was nearby and witnessed his approach. Though I was amused, a part of me was uncomfortable, and Bud picked up on this. He motioned Miller aside, and whispering in his ear, gently informed him of his mistake. When I took off my wig, Miller laughed and said, "Son of a gun!" Then we shook hands.

That might have been the end of it, but Val Lauder, who worked for the old Chicago Daily News, was there, and had witnessed the entire scene. She thought it was newsworthy. She featured it in her column "Keen Teens," headline and all. Her punch line was, "Baby, it was cold outside, but it became very warm inside for Johnny Miller when he discovered his mistake."

Another Star in the Family

One day, in the spring of the year, I brought my kid sister Sylvia with me for something called "A Taste of High School for Squirts," a day set aside for the expressed purpose of bringing your kid brother or sister to school. It was a good idea, I felt, because it seemed to make the transition from elementary school to high school smoother and not so intimidating. Sylvia was in grade five at the time.

The day went fine. Sylvia was even able to help me find some answers in a couple of my classes. She was a bright kid who didn't quite realize how bright she really was.

I had been asked to audition for, and was chosen for a lead part in the senior play some weeks earlier, and the idea fascinated her.

"Can I go to play practice with you after school?" she asked. "I'll be quiet. I won't be any trouble. Can I, can I?"

"Of course you can," I said, and thought no more about it.

At play practice later that day, we were practicing a dance routine which seemed quite challenging for a few of the boys.

"We don't have it down yet," said Victoria Sandomier, the faculty sponsor of the play.

"Okay, let's do it again," she said.

The boys had been practicing it for days, and I was beginning to wonder if they'd ever get it together. In a moment of silence before starting the routine again, we heard the rhythmic footwork of the dance from a bit of a distance. We all turned to the corner of the room to see where it was coming from. We were astonished to see my sister, unaware that she was being watched, doing the routine perfectly from start to finish after watching it only once.

When she finished, we all applauded. She then noticed us

and, although somewhat embarrassed, nevertheless beamed a winsome smile.

As we gathered around her, she said in a contrite way, "I hope I didn't disturb your practice."

"Heavens, no," gushed Mrs. Sandomier. "I think we've got a diamond in the rough here, P.J.," she said to me.

"It runs in the family," I said most vainly, as if it were preposterous for anyone to think otherwise.

"We should have her lead this dance routine," said Bob Lakemacher, the principal's son, who had one of the leads in the play. "She's better than any of us."

"Do you think your parents would consider it?" asked Mrs. Sandomier, who knew a thing or two about finding a new star.

"I'm sure," I told her, "that my mom and dad would be delighted."

My sister beamed, and beamed some more. In fact, she could not wipe the smile off her face for the rest of that evening, even after we went home.

So it came to be that Sylvia Alengo, future Schurzite and proud sister to P.J. (Pal Joe), led the best dance sequence in the senior play that year and bowed to uproarious applause, making her brother proud and her mom and dad ecstatic.

The Picture Contest

One day a number of us were considering whether or not we deserved a day off from school. We rationalized that we had worked hard and had been a credit to ourselves, the school, the state, the country, etc. We decided to put it to a vote. The vote to give ourselves a day off was unanimous. Of course, the school officials were not notified of this. We cut school, clear and simple. Call it senioritis or whatever you want.

There were ten of us. We drove to Lake Michigan for a while, had lunch, then swam and suntanned until three-thirty. Then we went northwest on Milwaukee Avenue to near the city limits and decided to go into an arcade. After a while, John McClenden came up with an idea we all thought bordered on brilliant.

"Each of you," he said, "will go into the picture booth, close the curtain, stand on the seat, drop your pants and jockey shorts, and pose for a picture of your private parts." (That is to say, of that part of our anatomy about which we each expressed the utmost pride at that time in our young lives.) "Then write your names on the backside of the photos, give 'em to Cliff Kessem or Binky Gilbert, and they'll arrange 'em for display on one of the pinball machines, and we'll all vote for the best looking one of the bunch."

We never got around to determining what the prize would be, if any. We didn't even finish all the picture-taking. A guy named Ted Pruitt was the one in the group who, for some unknown reason, seemed to evoke most of the put-downs and was the butt of practical jokes of group members. I don't know why. Some people just seem to attract that kind of thing, just as some people seem to attract respect.

Ted was the third to have his picture taken. When we were certain he had dropped his pants and his jockey shorts, Cliff opened the curtain with a flourish for all to see, and yelled his imitation of the trumpet sound, so familiar when attention is being drawn to a feature presentation anywhere.

"TA-DAH!"

Poor Ted was totally surprised.

"Damn, what's going on?" he said. His eyes opened wide, his mouth fell open, his face got red, and he struggled vainly to pull his jockey shorts and pants up. In so doing, he tore them because they didn't come up over his knees and derriere with his first upward pull. Instead they snagged, causing him to lose his balance and topple off the seat onto the floor in as ungainly and graceless a fall as I'd seen in quite a while. He managed to get a nasty elbow scrape as well as a bruised knee. But even though Ted was in pain, we were laughing much too hard to take serious notice of that.

"Here's the winner and new champeen. Take a bow, Ted," said Cliff, who tried to say more, but it was lost as he burst into gales of laughter, as did the rest of us.

"Cliff, show a little respect," said John, who then doubled over laughing. Tears were now rolling down his face.

"I don't see how you guys have any friends, the way you treat people," Binky said before he burst into another spasm of laughter.

Somehow, after that, we never did finish the picture-taking and judging. The guys were too scared it would happen again— to them! I've occasionally thought maybe each of us could have done the picture-taking, on his own, taking the pictures to a class reunion sometime and follow through to the conclusion. My wife Elaine, a breathtakingly level-headed woman, says no, but even though she's usually right about sensitive matters, there's a small part of me that thinks it would be fun.

First Snowfall

The first snowfall of the year, in late November, was truly beautiful. The flakes fell gently but abundantly, and soon the ground, streets, trees, and rooftops were cloaked in white. The scene would have done justice to a Christmas card.

Earl Strong, Frank Kubon, and I were having a cup of coffee and filling an hour between classes at the local tearoom near Chicago's Wright Junior College, enjoying each other's company. Frank, being the artistic one among us, was pointing out the beauty of the scene. I was content to simply watch and enjoy it. But Earl had other ideas. "Let's take a snow ride in my car," he offered.

We accepted. As we traveled the side streets, we skidded harmlessly as we turned a corner.

"Hey, that was fun!" exclaimed Earl. "Let's do it again."

"Yeah, let's," encouraged Frank who, artistic or not, appreciated excitement as much as the next guy—maybe more.

I remained quiet, alone in the back seat, until we skidded around three more corners. Then I said, "Maybe we shouldn't be doing this."

"It's okay, P.J.," Earl said. "I won't skid around any corners where there are cars parked, so we won't hit any."

"But Earl, someone might be walking, and you'll hit him..."

"Relax, P.J. Gotta get up some speed here so we can skid faster."

"Yeah, get up some speed, Earlie," encouraged Frank.

"Come on, you guys," I pleaded. "Something's going to happen."

Four more corners were approached and turned with increasing speed. The skids, even when we went into or climbed a curb, were harmless, because no cars were parked there. Soon we were all laughing.

We had gotten up some speed and had skidded merrily around a corner when it happened. We were sliding toward a lamp post.

"Oh, shit, who put that lamp post there?" said Earl excitedly as he tried to veer his vehicle to the left of it.

"Hey, maybe we'll miss it," laughed Frank.

"Get outta there, post," I yelled.

Crunch! It was the right front fender. We sat there laughing for a while. Then the three of us got out to check the damage. The entire fender and some of the grill were smashed. We all fell silent for a moment.

Then Earl said very softly, in self-reproach, "That's what you get for fuckin' around, Earl." Then again a little louder, "That's what you get for fuckin' around, Earl!" Again and again he said it, each time louder, until he was shouting as loud as he could, "THAT'S WHAT YOU GET FOR FUCKIN' AROUND, EARL!"

Frank and I were laughing through all of this, and soon Earl joined us. Anyone passing by might have mistaken us for lunatics, and at that moment they might have been right.

Soon we were shopping the local auto repair shops for damage estimates, with Earl explaining that "a post hit me."

Sneaking into the Movie

One night six of us, the starting varsity basketball five and our sixth man, decided we needed a little adventure to keep our minds alert and for the general appreciation of living which it offers. We met at Frank Miller's house. He lived in the Logan Square area, and he said it would be easy to sneak into the local movie theater on Milwaukee Avenue, a main shopping drag.

"Just follow me, you guys."

We followed him into a gangway. He stopped under a fire escape, jumped up, and grabbed the unit which contained the last few stairs, and it slid down to the ground, ready to use.

"Follow me," he whispered.

I felt like James Cagney outwitting the police. He took us up one story and stopped at a window which was barely open about an inch. He motioned for us to lie low and keep quiet.

"Shh," he said. He kept looking into the small space the partially open window provided. It seemed he looked forever, and some of us giggled.

Finally, he said, "Okay, all clear," and opened the window and climbed in. We had some big boys, so we opened the window quite a lot. I was the smallest. We had some studs, and as a group we presented, physically, quite a formidable sight, especially dressed in blue jeans, sweatshirts, and the like, not exactly what the well behaved, mild-mannered gentlemen were wearing.

After hurriedly climbing inside, we found we were in the women's restroom, one of several ways Frank often chose to enter and enjoy one of Hollywood's offerings when he did not want to deplete his pockets of any money.

One of the doors to a toilet stall opened and a middle-aged woman appeared as shocked and surprised at seeing six motley-looking young men in a women's restroom as anyone I have ever seen. Fenny, a guy who fancied himself a lady's man, smiled at her in what he thought was his most charming and charismatic manner and took a step toward her.

"It's all right, ma'am—"

Before he could finish his opening line, she responded with the most frightening scream I have ever heard.

My good pal, Raffe Simonian, an all-conference player, exercised his athletic agility by flying out the window. So did another two pals, Jim Brahm and Max Saxinger. Max's red hair was matched now by his embarrassed, frightened face. Fenny, whom many thought to be a bit on the slow side on the court, proved his critics wrong as he moved out the door and into the theater with extraordinary quickness. So did Frank and I.

I believe that we were more frightened than that woman. I remember having hurriedly seated myself in the middle of an empty row near the back of the theater. I had no idea where the others were. I sat with my eyes transfixed on the screen, not daring to look sideways at the usher who seemed very suspicious. He came by several times, looking me over.

I remember Turhan Bay, a journeyman horror-movie actor, playing the same role he always played in horror movies. This was one about a mummy's curse. That movie didn't scare me nearly as much as that lady's scream. I'll bet she could have made a lot of money screaming in horror movies.

Wright On

For those of us who don't have big bucks, a junior college close to home can be a good choice. Wright Junior College on Chicago's northwest side had the makings of a good freshman and sophomore foundation, if you took advantage of the situation. By the time I registered, I knew I wanted to teach. After Wright, I would transfer to Northern Illinois University.

"I want you to give a two-minute speech of an interesting personal experience," said Henry Link, instructor of Speech I, my first class of the day. "I promise we won't laugh or otherwise embarrass you, but remember, you have to believe in what you're saying. That'll go a long way in persuading all of us to believe it. We're all friends, here."

He looked at us with an expression of such sincerity that it was doubtful anyone would disbelieve him. His smile was soft and seemed to inspire confidence in his class members, even though this was the first day of class.

"Are there any shy people in this class?" Link asked. "It's not such a bad thing to be shy, but I'm hoping you can shed it when you're giving a speech. I think this class can help you. We'll have several different types of speech situations, and you can assume a different identity, and thus shed your shyness. I've seen it happen," he said.

He was right. By the middle of the semester we witnessed Carolyn Hart, the shyest girl I've ever met, doing a wonderful version of "Casey at the Bat," wearing a baseball hat slightly sideways, and with terrific voice inflections and gestures. I'll always remember how uplifting it felt for me watching and listening to her.

"...And when the dust had lifted, and they saw what had occurred, there was Jimmy safe at second"—arms and hands were energetically giving the safe gesture—"and Flynn was a-huggin third"—her right arm was hooked to an imaginary base."

Then, "Casey, mighty Casey, was advancing to the bat." I was mesmerized. I was a convert of Henry Link, with a huge assist from Carolyn Hart. Yes, there is nothing comparable to the joy of young minds awakening.

The social studies department included an energetic group.

"We're planning a mock Republican Presidential Convention," said Dr. Brian Bradley, "but before that, the social studies department is challenging the school baseball team to a softball game. We know we'll be victorious."

The game was a tongue-in-cheek challenge which was quickly accepted. Of course the school baseball team won, without having to exert much energy, but the feeling of fun and friendship helped create a relaxed atmosphere for the convention. The theme (this was before the actual Republican convention) turned out to be "I like Ike, but I like Taft better." Taft won Wright Junior College's Republican nomination.

Even though history would soon prove the error of our crystal ball, the mock convention was a huge success, and fun too.

Dr. Phil Lanthrop captured our spirit of fun in his physical science class. Having some difficulty getting our attention focused on an explanation of some igneous rocks at the start of one of his classes, he said, typically, with an engaging smile, "Listen here. Stop talking; I've got rocks here."

We cheerfully laughed, and gave him our complete attention.

I found Wright Junior College to be a fine school with a fine staff. I became a serious student and was able to earn good grades. Every department was quite good.

There was even a sponsorship of an outstanding jazz band, begun by some motivated student musicians, and encouraged and sponsored by, yes, the social studies department. A concert they gave, free of charge, was first rate.

Because of the humanities department, I came to appreciate W. Somerset Maugham, F. Scott Fitzgerald, Ernest Hemingway, and others.

One of the sad things was that there were a large number of kids attending Wright who were wasting their time, their teachers' time, and sometimes their fellow students' time. They seemed immature and aimless. It was usually only a matter of time before many of them flunked out. Take Jerry Stevens, for instance.

"P.J., let's cut our two last classes and go horseback riding."

"No, Jerry, I have to study for the physical science test Friday."

"But it's only Wednesday. Plenty of time."

Or "Are you going to the Dave Brubeck concert?"

"That's in the middle of the week."

"But P.J., it's un-American to not attend. How would you explain it to people?" Jerry flunked out after one semester, one of many who did.

Wright was a good place. If you could resist the temptation to get lazy, cut class, and skip assignments, you could get through the first two years of college at a reasonable cost by living at home. There was one problem, however. For some reason, when a junior college student transferred to a four-year school, often he would wind up being a few credits short. I don't know why that was. Perhaps that has been corrected by this time. But I still think it was a bargain.

I played basketball at Wright. I loved the game too much to give it up. I remember a road trip over a weekend. Friday night we had a conference game at LaSalle-Peru Junior College, and Saturday we were in Peoria to play against Bradley's junior varsity as a preliminary to their varsity game. Bradley was tops in the country. They recruited some of the best players. Recruit may not be the right word. No, they didn't really recruit; they selected.

Many good high-school players wanted to be in Bradley's basketball program. I remember that they kicked the hell out of us. We all knew Barry Goldman, one of their starting guards, who had been one of the best players in the city in high school, and he wasn't regarded as their best ballplayer. People from miles around followed Bradley. They were nuts about Bradley basketball.

We were staying at the Jefferson Hotel, two to a room. Earlier that Saturday, in the later afternoon, our phone rang. It was Bob Reda, a teammate.

"Get your uniforms on, just the shorts and jersey top, no long warmup pants or jackets. Coach told me to call. Local paper wants some team pictures," he said.

So Max Saxinger and I dressed, left the room, and boarded the elevator. It isn't every day that someone in a basketball uniform uses a hotel elevator, and people looked at us with considerable curiosity. We felt self-conscious. When we reached the lobby it was quite crowded, and we could feel several more people looking at us. We looked around for the photographer, but couldn't see one. There were no teammates in basketball uniforms—nothing. We'd been tricked.

Then we spotted Bob across the lobby, laughing. We took off after him. "Wait'll we get you, you bastard," I yelled. He ran out the door, with Max and me in fervent pursuit.

"You'll never live to tell this story, you SOB," Max snarled.

Bob and I ran around the corner. Max dropped out of the race. I began to shiver. I was then startled with the realization that it was five degrees above zero, and here I was in this little basketball uniform. Bob was wearing a toasty-warm overcoat.

"We're locking you out of the hotel. I hope you freeze your balls off," I yelled, and ran back to the warmth of the hotel.

Your Buddy, J.C.

Northern Illinois University, at that time, was a small school, with an enrollment of around fifteen hundred, and just beginning to expand in the little sleepy town of DeKalb, Illinois. Presently it has in the neighborhood of fifty thousand students. They've added a new football stadium, a new fieldhouse with new basketball courts, track, offices, and classrooms, and several buildings. I went back recently while visiting friends in DeKalb and I didn't recognize the place. I'm glad I attended when I did. I'd be uncomfortable with the big crowds there today.

I lived in a private home with four other guys, as there were not enough dormitories at the time. One of my roommates was Dick Bartels, straight as can be, scornful of any slight hint of pomposity or phoniness, and rather surprisingly irreverent.

"You think going to church is going to wipe out all the sins of the week before? What a copout. Personal responsibility is where it's at," he'd say.

"You should come to church with me," I'd say.

"I don't believe in God. That's for weaklings who lack personal accountability. If it will make you happy, you can pray for me," he'd say.

Above his bed was a picture of Jesus which was autographed in the lower right corner. "Dear Dick: To a great guy . . . . Your buddy, J.C."

If he were asked whether or not that was sacrilegious, Dick would say "I believe there was a Jesus Christ, but I don't believe he was the savior of mankind. But he seemed to be well adjusted, considering he was an only child and all."

A few years later Dick headed west to Fresno, California. My wife Elaine, and I spent some time with him and Sam, his wife.

He taught history at a nearby college, but didn't earn a great deal of money. He did it because he liked it. He and a partner made a good deal of money building in-ground swimming pools. At the time we visited them, Dick and his partner were getting out of the swimming pool business. Curious, I asked why.

"I'm spending too much time in court. Oftentimes, we'll finish one third of the work and get paid for it, then finish the second third and get paid for it, but in many cases, after we finish the last third, these people say they're not going to pay, and suggest we take them to court, hoping we wouldn't bother. We did bother, and now I've had a bellyful, and I'm getting out of the business."

I found it interesting (and discouraging) that this non-religious man was in many ways a better person than many of those who espoused religion.

Uncle Sam Wants You

After finishing college at Northern Illinois University, I received my official draft notice in late March 1956. At the draft station in Chicago on Van Buren Street I saw a lot of guys I knew who had also recently graduated from college. The old sarge walked into the large crowded room with our names on a clipboard, said the Navy was drafting that month as well as the Army, that when he called out our names, we were to shout out "Army" or "Navy" and they'd do their best to grant our preferences. He gave us ten minutes to think about it.

"What'cha gonna do, Pal Joe?" some of the guys asked me.

"Are you kidding? I'm going Navy. Fight the battle, and when it's over, you take a shower. No slipping and sliding in dirt and foxholes for me, boys."

"Yeah, sounds good, Pal Joe."

All of the group I gathered with went Navy. Since, surprisingly, most of the guys outside our circle chose Army, the Navy choices stood up.

We went through the physical, then boarded a bus and were taken to Great Lakes Naval Training Station in North Chicago where we were given a second physical, then to the barber who shaved each head bald, then the quartermaster who issued our uniforms.

"I've seen better heads on flat beer," he said.

Then came the first day of boot camp.

"I'm Mr. Amos, 'sir,'" growled our new company commander, the first words he spoke to us. "Is that clear?"

"Yes, sir," said a few of us who were not completely intimidated, barely audibly.

"I can't hear you," growled Mr. Amos.

"Yes, sir!" we all shouted in unison.

"That's more like it," he grinned. "There might be some hope for you assholes in this canoe club. Remember, you are the lowest thing around. You salute everything in a uniform except for assholes"—he loved to use that word— "like yourselves." Though he said that not much in this modern navy surprised him anymore, he seemed at least mildly surprised, and we thought we recognized a hint of a grin at the corners of his mouth when our entire company saluted the uniformed Coca-Cola man as we marched by one day.

"We have these assholes well trained," he advised the Coke man. We very rarely heard Mr. Amos speak in other than a growl, but most of us grew to at least tolerate, if not love him.

We were, for the most part, a draftee company, and most of the draftees were recent college graduates. We were intelligent and we knew how to take tests, which were administered once each week. We scored the highest of all companies each week for several weeks, and were entitled to carry the "I" flag as we marched from place to place around the base.

"We may not look like we're doing much, but we're an intelligent bunch of bastards," Mr. Amos would growl proudly to a friend as our company marched down the street. After all the tests were administered near the end of boot camp, Mr. Amos informed us that we, Company 261, had tied the record for the highest overall scoring average in the base's history.

"I'm proud of you assholes," he said. We all cheered and laughed. Mr. Amos laughed, too.

Gene Tomaszek, a friend from elementary school, became a close friend in boot camp. He was a baseball fan and a good player himself. He littered his speech with phrases having to do with baseball. "It's a beautiful day for a ball game. Let's play two today," or, "Good show, a circuit clout," or, "Where've you been; we missed your big bat in the lineup, kid," etc.

One night after lights were out, some of the guys were talking in the clerk's room, a short way from the main sleeping quarters. Someone carelessly flicked a cigarette into a huge carton of popcorn someone else's mother had sent. From my bunk I smelled the smoke and I went immediately to Gene's bunk.

"I think there's a fire in the clerk's room, Gene."

"So you're in trouble, and you've come to me, the great relief pitcher, to put out the fire," he said.

"Fan the sumbitch before it goes out," came the advice from the next bunk.

Of three water buckets always readied for such emergencies, I grabbed one, and in my haste, I kicked and tripped over a second, losing the contents of both.

"I've gotcha covered," yelled Gene, and he grabbed the remaining bucket and put out the fire. We were relieved. No one doubted that in a very short time the barracks would have been lost.

"I expect a nomination for MVP," said Gene, grinning.

We were so busy in boot camp that we scarcely realized the weeks went by so fast. It seemed that when we looked up it was June, and soon boot camp would be over.

We were happy the weather was warm. It was Saturday. We were left alone with no company commander. Most of us would strip off our white uniforms in the barracks so that we could wear them for two days.

I was sound asleep in my bunk when I was awakened by the roar of fifty-nine sailors answering "yes" to the question, "Do you want to give P.J. a GI shower?"

A GI shower is given with scrub brushes and is most uncomfortable. I was the recruit company commander in Mr. Amos's absence, and it had become a custom at Great Lakes to give sailors with my rank one of these showers near the end of boot camp.

They grabbed me by my arms and legs. My struggling proved fruitless. I decided to relax until we reached a point where the stairs were, then I would leap out of their grasp. It was worth a try. At that moment I leaped free of their grasp, and I could scarcely believe my good luck. I jumped to a landing halfway down, and took another leap to the ground floor and out the door.

I ran around a corner at the end of the block, and walking toward me was an officer. Not knowing quite what to do, I saluted him, and in his surprise, he saluted me back. A moment later the rest of Company 261 came around the corner. They stopped and retreated back to the barracks with the officer in pursuit.

I decided to get back to the barracks. The officer was there.

"It's my fault, sir. I told him his girlfriend was ugly," I lied, pointing to Gene Tomaszek.

"You guys are all on report," the officer told us. Then he left. We decided to phone Mr. Amos.

"What'd you assholes do?" he asked. We told him. Mr. Amos had a good laugh. He didn't seem to be worried. "They'll order you down to battalion headquarters, give you a good chewing out, and threaten you with having to repeat boot camp. You guys look sorry and act like good little assholes, and I'll make a phone call or two and see if I still have any influence in this canoe club."

"You men are a disgrace to the United States Navy," roared the officer on duty a little later at battalion headquarters. "Who ever told you you were fit to wear the uniform? We'll be looking closer into this matter. It's likely you'll have to repeat boot camp. If that happens, you'll be getting off easy. If it were up to me, I'd put you in jail for three months before repeating boot camp."

Even though Mr. Amos said these things were unlikely, we still came away contrite and badly shaken.

Nothing more was ever said of the incident. The end of our term in boot camp came, and we did not have to repeat it. Not a man among us ever brought it up, as if bringing it up would cause the threat to come true.

Battle Stations

A large part of my hitch in the U.S. Navy took place on the USS Stark County, an LST whose home port was Pearl Harbor, Hawaii.

I first came aboard one day in September at 1630 (that's 4:30 p.m.) and we left port at 1700, bound for Maui. We were nearing Maui the next morning. In the distance there were some ships, and aircraft could be seen. But that's not an unusual sight, and we paid no attention to it.

Suddenly, "General quarters, battle stations" exploded over the public address system. "This is not a drill! All hands, battle stations!"

"Good grief, Pearl Harbor sneak attack all over again," I thought. The chief petty officer across the hall came running out and banged hard against our personnel office Dutch door. His red face and excited expression indicated he'd been at war before. People were running everywhere I looked. Rex Clark, the other sailor working in the personnel office, started running, presumably to his battle station, and I ran behind him. Because I had just come aboard minutes before leaving Pearl Harbor the day before, no one had yet told me where my battle station was. I figured I'd help Rex wherever he went.

In my excitement I ran too fast—ran on the back of his legs, to be exact. He went down in a belly flop with me on top of him. He turned to look up. He had been unaware that I was following him. When he realized I was, he exclaimed, "What the hell are you doing?"

"I'm following you because I don't know where my battle station is."

"Don't follow me," shouted Rex. "I'm up on the bridge with

the captain, the most dangerous spot on the ship; I'm his telephone talker."

Not knowing where to go, I headed back to the personnel office. After a time the "All clear" sounded, and we went to our usual places. It turned out that a young sailor, seventeen, had checked the (gun) powder room as he was going about his daily chores, and the temperature there had seemed dangerously high. He ran to the microphone at the quarterdeck and called "battle stations"— "Abandon ship," maybe, but "battle stations"? The captain gave him a good chewing out. Then we all had a good laugh about it, but we were all grateful it had been a false alarm and not the real thing.

In the meantime, I was shown my battle station. I was to go up to the bridge, then climb a ladder to a spot called "the Crow's Nest," open a large box filled with pennant-type flags there, of every color and color combination imaginable. A certain one of these flags is a battle flag, and I was instructed to "fly the battle flag."

When I think about it, I can't help but smile. Imagine being bombed, strafed, and torpedoed, with firepower exploding everywhere. I have to fly a flag to let the world know we're in battle?

Happy Birthday

I came to be employed by my school district fresh out of the Navy. I was put to work the day after I was hired, near the end of January, which seemed a bit unusual. Most teachers finish out the school year, or if there's an illness, a substitute is hired, usually until the end of a marking period. I was too overjoyed to be getting a real job in my chosen work to give it any except a passing thought.

I soon learned that there had been three other teachers that year before me: the regular teacher who started the school year, and two others who had tried valiantly, but had quit with considerable anger. The superintendent, Glenn Westlake, a man of stature and charm in the community, had to sweet-talk the last one into staying until he signed me up. The scuttlebutt was that the regular teacher who started the year had given it a good try, but the kids had driven her bonkers. She reportedly became so ill, "emotionally," the rumors had it, that she couldn't return. The other two just gave it up before they got that way.

These were junior high eighth-graders, old enough to be "feeling their oats," but not smart enough to know when to back off. Then I came. I'm sure the kids thought I'd be gone in a matter of weeks. These weren't knife-wielding, gun-toting kids, but they were outrageous. They sassed back, they cut class, they took doors off their hinges, etc. Of course, they hadn't learned a thing. Most of them didn't know a noun from a first down— On second thought, they did know what a first down was. They needed discipline. I had gravely underestimated the size of my task. They had never told us about these things in those college education courses. They have you believing that every kid wants to learn and there are no problems. They don't know the real world.

Clearly, the person in this situation had to be naive, or so motivated to teach that these obstacles could be overcome. I was a combination of these. I was still naive enough to believe that there are no bad kids, and I was so happy about having my military obligation over (though I did recognize it as a good experience), that it seemed nothing could be done to seriously discourage me. I was truly happy to be there. Oh, we had our moments, and I went around and around with some of these kids, but I loved them all, and they seemed to pick this up.

There were no grudges held. Occasionally, I became a bit rough in my disciplinary measures, even though I'd heard it rumored that the superintendent didn't want his teachers using corporal punishment. One day, Jim Burke (not his real name), a rascal who had been testing my patience, pulled a chair out from behind another boy when he went to sit in it. I not-so-gently informed Jim that his next cheap trick would be met with a genuine old-fashioned, across-my-knee spanking. Guess what? It happened again the next day, and the class eagerly reminded me of my promise to spank him. They were tired of that stuff, too! I put Jim over my knee, began giving him a few good shots on his backside when the door opened, and there stood Mr. Glenn Westlake, Superintendent of Schools, who, it was said, did not want his teachers using corporal punishment!

I couldn't believe it. I had to think fast, or my career here was over when I was barely getting started, I thought. The Almighty must have felt pity for me, and He delivered an idea which, in an instant, came full-blown in my mind. I whacked Jim's backside once more, then paused and said, "And one for good luck," whacked him again, put him on his feet, gave him a gentle shove in the direction of his seat, and said cheerily, "Happy birthday, Jim!"

The class members picked up the intent of this charade instantly, and laughed and clapped and wished Jim happy birthday, too. Mr. Westlake, meanwhile, smiled benignly. This seemingly warm, happy scene was something of which he approved. He whispered a message in my ear momentarily. Would I stop by his office after school to sign a routine form they had overlooked in my contract-signing a few days earlier? I said I would. I would have shined his shoes, poured his coffee, washed his car, anything he asked. Then he left, still smiling that pleased, benign smile. When the door closed behind him, all of us, every class member, Jim included, laughed for what seemed like several minutes, but in reality could not have been more than three or four. That incident, without a doubt, brought us all closer together. It formed a cohesiveness between them and me and one another, which wasn't there before. We discovered we truly liked each other, and from that point there followed more kindness, more consideration, and more genuine learning.

The Incorrigible

Jerry Pankowicz was a tough kid to please. For starters, he hadn't done a lick of schoolwork since he entered school in kindergarten. He had skipped school quite a bit, starting as early as third grade. He was a big kid, and consequently became a bully, often hurting other kids for no good reason.

If he took a disliking to a teacher, it seemed nothing that teacher could do would please him. He had been passed from grade to grade, something called a "social promotion," meaning he didn't fulfill the work requirements but was too big to be held back. At the junior high school, Jerry hated his language arts teacher. He wanted to be in Mrs. Phyllis Burckle's class. He had Mrs. Burckle for homeroom, and largely through her efforts, they got along just fine.

It would seem to follow that if a change in his program was to be made, he'd be placed in her class, right? Not necessarily. Bill Chessnut, the principal, didn't want Jerry to have his own way entirely. He changed his program so that he'd get half of what he wanted. Jerry wanted out of his present language arts class. Okay, but he was not placed in Phyllis Burckle's class. He liked me, but not as much as he liked Phyllis, and so he was placed in my language arts class. The program change necessitated his also being in one of my physical education classes in the middle of the school day at lunchtime.

"I forgot my gym suit at home," Jerry would say, then disappear.

I told him he'd have to stay with the class.

"Okay, okay," said Jerry.

It was spring, and we were outside; he could umpire one of the softball games. He'd stick around for a few days, then he'd disappear again.

"I had to run to the store to buy some loose-leaf paper," he'd say.

I told him if he didn't stick around I'd have to report it to the principal, who wanted to know everything that was going on with Jerry. He stuck around for a couple more days, then began disappearing again.

I told Principal Bill Chessnut. Chessnut was upset. He brought Jerry into his office.

"We've tried to take care of you, but you won't meet us halfway. I'm suspending you for the rest of the school year, and you won't graduate with your class." There was only one week left of school. A phone call to his mother advised her of the consequences. Jerry appeared to be badly shaken.

On the night of graduation, I caught sight of Jerry hanging around the playground. When I returned to my car after graduation, I found the right front tire flat. A spike had been driven through it. I changed it, putting on the spare. The next evening as I was driving on the Eisenhower Interstate, the left front tire went flat. A closer look at the tire revealed that a spike had been driven into it as well, but hadn't quite made it through. Riding at relatively high speed on it had been enough to make it go flat.

I reported it to Bill Chessnut, who refused to believe that Jerry would do such a thing.

"Oh well, you win a few and you lose a few," I said, but argued that Jerry was capable of doing this thing.

About eight or nine years later, Jerry's friend, Thor Janson, who had become a butcher at the local food store, told Phyllis Burckle, "Jerry really did puncture Mr. Alengo's car tires with an ice pick." Thor, a grade behind Jerry, was with him when he did the deed.

Andy and the Speech Correctionist

Andy Magoo (not his real name) was a man's man, one of those men who doesn't particularly appeal to many women because he is so masculine that he seems to lack culture and refinement, and whose behavior thus appears to border on coarse and even vulgar. He was the kind of guy whose integrity, honesty, and sense of humor would be stoutly defended by many husbands, whose wives quite openly volunteered their distaste for his tactless, base personality traits.

Of course, it was true. Andy was about as subtle as a dump truck. Brutally and tactlessly honest, he sometimes made even strong men wince when he used some very blue language in his directness.

But the guys on the faculty loved him. There was a humor in his tactlessness and, more important, in a business where politics and deceit sometimes play a part in advancement in one's career, Andy was without guile, straight as an arrow, a threat to no one. Andy was as close to comic Don Rickles as anyone I've known. To most men Andy was refreshing, someone who, despite his lack of sophistication, had a certain character beneath the roughness to be admired. He was a thoroughbred of sorts, a one of a kind.

Andy was a junior high shop teacher, and the boys in his classes (this was before girls could take shop) loved him, too. Funny thing about kids: Sometimes they seem to sense whether or not someone is really a good person. He handled the boys very well. He'd give them hell when they had it coming, but then it was over. He held no grudges. Further, he had a good sense of what was important to discipline and what wasn't. He often winked at some minor, unimportant misbehavior which some others might focus on with major attention. The boys in his classes recognized this as a strength, not a weakness, and in the meantime, they were able to focus their attention on the tasks at hand, feeling secure with their leader, having a sense that all was right in that little corner of the world.

One day, near the beginning of the school year Patsy Wickers, a speech correctionist, whose duties were transferred that year from elsewhere in the district to the junior high, was making rounds. Patsy was a girl with a pretty face, and a figure which would help sell a lot of magazines if she were to pose for the cover. She liked to wear tight skirts and sweaters, and conversations between men would stop when she came into view, and would be resumed only when she was out of sight. Women staff members, interestingly enough, seemed cool toward her. In the course of her rounds, Patsy knocked on the shop door. Andy opened it and looked upon Patsy as she stood directly before his attentive eyes, in all her glory. Andy smiled and looked at her from the top of her head to the soles of her shoes, then into her eyes.

"Do you have any stutterers?" Patsy asked.

"I-I-I don-don-don't kn-kn-know," replied Andy, still smiling at her.

Patsy slammed the door in his still smiling face, turned on her heel, and walked quickly away.

Nice play, Andy.

The Repapswen

When I was teaching sixth grade, beginning in September 1963, I had a newspaper unit, and the class and I published a class newspaper. The form of the verb "publish" is used loosely here. The kids wrote their stories longhand, and I typed them on mimeo stencils (no copy machines at that time). I have a bit of a lifelong love affair with writing and journalism—maybe I was a frustrated writer—and, in talking with the class about a newspaper unit, I was able to use my own enthusiasm for it to get them motivated and fired up. Oftentimes, when you say "newspaper" to sixth-graders, they look upon it as some vague, gray, dull, and adult kind of thing which couldn't possibly have any relevance to them at the time. But as part of my motivational planning, I would make a reference to a movie or a TV show. I'd even mention that Superman's cover was that of Clark Kent, reporter with partner Lois Lane at the Daily Planet. This would suddenly make the subject of a newspaper more interesting. Soon class members would recall the shows in our discussions, and I knew I was meeting with some success in getting them motivated. At a given point I would become more underhanded and share with them some exciting moments from my own days as a young, crackerjack newspaperman, all of which were from very creative and imaginative stories I had dreamed up, of course, because I had never earned a living as a journalist.

"Ah, I remember my days as a sportswriter with the Chicago Tribune," I'd say. In my self-styled logic of justice, I excused these little white lies because they served to motivate the kids into some good work. Liars of the world, arise; you can do so much good in the world!

When the kids had been manipulated to a point at which I felt satisfied, I'd go into my academy-award act to get them to ask—no, beg is a better word—for permission to have a class newspaper. I'd say something like, "You know, I've been thinking—No, it's a crazy idea; forget it..."

"What, Mr. Alengo? Tell us," they'd say.

"No, I don't think you can handle it. It's too ambitious. You're too young," I'd say.

"We can do it! Tell us!" They didn't even know what I had in mind yet, but they were sure they could do it.

I knew I had them now. "I shouldn't have said anything. You'd only laugh. It was foolish of me to even think of it. We'd better get out our math books and get to our next assignment."

"Mr. Alengo, please."

"I guess I better tell you, or you won't concentrate on math until I do. I was thinking of a class newspaper—news of class happenings, sports coverage of interschool rivalry, recipes, feature stories about class members, teachers, and stuff like that. It's a lot of hard work, and we can't do it until we've finished, I mean really learned, the newspaper unit. Would you like me to invite a professional journalist from the Tribune, a good friend of mine, to talk to you about his experiences?" I asked them.

Yes, they would like that. I had in mind my old friend and teammate, Max Saxinger, who first wrote on the sports pages, then handled straight news. He was a good journalist, and, I'm sorry to say, died of a heart attack in 1997. Max came and talked to all of my classes. All it cost me was a spaghetti dinner I talked my wife into preparing. Not bad for all the journalistic smarts and savvy to which he treated us.

From that point, I made it appear that my classes were persuading me into a class newspaper. Sometimes I thought I was in the wrong business, that I should have been a salesman or, better yet, a con man. I'd be rich, I tell you, rich!

We had fun with the newspaper unit, and occasionally I would even become democratic about some aspects of it. For

67

example, I allowed the class to nominate and vote for the name of our class newspaper. You'd always get the usual nominations: the Tribune, the Bugle, the Spotlighter, etc., but occasionally someone would think creatively and come up with something imaginative. In some of their less happy moments the kids would refer to the name of the school, which was Pleasant Lane, as "Prison Pain," so one brilliant kid one year nominated Prison Pain Patter as the name of our newspaper. Having begun the exercise in a spirit of democracy, I could not suddenly become autocratic and forbid it, and so, after the votes were counted, Prison Pain Patter was the unanimous choice.

But I think the best one came a year or two later from Kris Ekvall, a cute, shy, but clever little girl. When I called on her for her contribution to the nominations for the name of our class newspaper, she replied "Repapswen," from her seat at the front of the class.

"Repapswen?" I asked.

"Umhum," she replied, nodding her cute little blond head.

"What's Repapswen?" I asked, screwing up my face into the contortions of one who is completely bewildered.

"That's newspaper, spelled backwards," she said, triumphantly turning her head toward the class for their approval. She had no trouble coaxing them. They were delighted. They laughed, they mugged, they guffawed.

"My mother told me there'd be days like this," I said, covering my face with my hands. "She tried to tell me to get a nice little chicken farm. Why didn't I listen to her?"

And so it came to pass that the name of our class newspaper that year, by unanimous vote, was the Repapswen.

Me and My Shadow

Sooner or later with sixth-graders or junior-high kids, a discussion about pets would come about. It might happen during or after an oral book report, or even as a digression from a subject-matter discussion.

I often allowed this to happen, because most kids love to talk about their pets. Actually most people, young or old, like to talk about their pets. With sixth-graders, talking about them builds in many of them a self-confidence which may have been lacking when discussing more scholarly things.

Invariably, I'd be asked if I had a pet as a boy or if I presently had one, and would I tell them about it. That's when I'd go into my story about my childhood pet, a black cocker spaniel named Shadow.

"Shadow was a very bright, intelligent, and lively dog. We did many things together. He was a fast learner. He could fetch a thrown stick, catch a frisbee, shake hands, roll over, play dead, sit up on command, get my slippers—just about anything you could think of. There seemed to be nothing he couldn't learn."

"One evening a few years later, when I was a young man and I was going out for a night on the town, I asked Shadow to get me a white dress shirt. He had never done this before, and I was curious as to whether or not he could do it. As I was shaving, I could hear some activity from the direction of my bedroom. When I finished, I went to my bedroom and there was Shadow, sewing a button on my shirt!"

Class members recognized immediately that they'd been duped, but we all had a good laugh about it. They would refer to Shadow often during the course of the school year, sometimes as a confidence-builder: "If Shadow can learn to sew buttons on shirts, we can learn about predicate adjectives."

A more recent pet was Kirby, originally spelled Curby, being

69

short for "Curbstone Setter," the vernacular for a pooch of so many breeds that no one breed seems dominant. We figured that changing the spelling of his name would lend him a measure of dignity and charm. Kirby was acquired for my children, Dave and Cindy. Though of dubious ancestry, he was nonetheless lively, a lot of fun, and, I thought, quite intelligent. He did the usual fetching of thrown sticks, and tricks which many dogs do, but there is one little gem which I believe was singularly his. Cindy would take him with her when she went jogging, a ritual she performed regularly for fitness purposes. After their return home, both Cindy and Kirby would be exhausted and immediately seek relief through resting—Cindy on the couch, and Kirby on the floor.

One day they started their jogging ritual as usual, but when Cindy turned the corner at the end of the block, Kirby turned around and came back home.

We all thought he was pretty smart to have thought about it and to have decided not to do it. Upon her return, after jogging the full distance, Cindy playfully scolded him while the rest of us laughed and kidded her good-naturedly that the dog was smarter than she was.

Kirby also became a scapegoat of sorts, taking the blame for one thing or another. "Who ate the rest of that pie in the refrigerator?" When no family member would admit to it, we'd say, "It must have been Kirby."

I told that story in class one day, and after that, if someone in class did something and I'd ask, for example, "who had taken the basketball from the closet," usually a class member would say, "Kirby did it," before another class member would say, "I have it, Mr. A. It wasn't Kirby this time."

Some incidents might well have turned ugly had they not been defused by the "Kirby did it" phrase. I shall always be grateful to my four-legged friends.

Is It the Pen That's Mightier than the Sword?

One of the things we decided as a class was that since we were going to be such a good newspaper staff, we would put samples of our work on display in a prominent part of the room. We decided the side wall near the front of the room was best. Upon entering the room from the hall, this display would then be the first thing a visitor would see.

Eric Hanson and Steve Young, a couple of very bright and personable boys, suggested that the old proverb "the pen is mightier than the sword" would be a perfect title for our display. They had read it in a book of proverbs in the reference section of our library. While the rest of the class was busy with some language arts seat work, Eric and Steve were taping the large all-capital letters of the title to the designated portion of the wall. The fire exit door on that side was about six feet from the front wall, so the display, and the title, had limited space. The title was going to have to be a two-liner: "The Pen Is" on one line, and "Mightier than the Sword" on the second line. I was so busy going from desk to desk helping class members with their language arts assignment that I hadn't noticed that Eric and Steve had finished the display title and returned to their seats (they finished everything fast!) to tackle the seat work.

Out of the corner of my eye, I saw the teacher from the classroom next door, Lona Lipton (whom the kids referred to as "Mrs. Teabag" when they thought they were out of earshot) in the hall, covering her face with her hands, trying to contain her laughter which seemed about to explode any second now into an absolute peal. She was looking at our newspaper display title. I quickly, but quietly, went into the hall to find out what I was missing.

"Look," she said, pointing to the title. Then covering her face again to contain her laughter.

I looked. The boys had not allowed nearly enough space between two words in the first line, and for some reason had put a long dash at the end of that line. The result was something I'm certain they had not intended:
THE PENIS —
MIGHTIER THAN THE SWORD

Now I was putting my hands to my face to contain my laughter. We didn't want to call attention to it, after all. After school that day, I climbed the stepladder, and spaced the letters correctly so that the intended meaning was communicated to all. Neither the class nor anyone else, save for Lona and me, were any the wiser.

Holiday Seasons to Remember

It is traditional in our school district to share the warm feelings of the holiday season with the local community. (We began calling it "holiday" instead of "Christmas" because some of our Jewish community members objected to the distinction strenuously.) We share it in a most pleasant and wholesome way by having the school children and their teachers produce and present a singing program. This is quite popular with the parents. The youngest participating children, the first-graders, are absolutely precious. They positively cannot do anything wrong! If they spot Mom or Aunt Minnie or Grandpa in the audience and wave, it's really cute as ever. They can stumble, scratch their faces, bump into the kids next to them—anything—it's okay. They're so innocent, so natural, they steal the show and your heart. Their singing is awful—they can't reach any high notes. But the audience loves it. The first-graders certainly are charmers, and they're not even trying to be.

For a holiday music show, all the kids look clean. Their clothes are clean and pressed, and their faces have that well-scrubbed look. They come close to looking angelic; if you look close, you can almost see the halos. Never mind that any number of them may have been fighting on the playground the previous days or rolling in the mud, or whatever. I remember one holiday program where the fifth and sixth grades combined for their song offerings. They stood on risers—that is, three tiered rows, each slightly higher than the one in front of it; it made for a good visual effect. But one tall, blond boy sported a black eye, which contrasted sharply with his fair complexion and hair. He was smack-dab in the middle of the entire group and immediately captured the amused attention of the audience. The scene looked to me like a Norman Rockwell painting on one of those old Saturday Evening Post magazine covers. Ah, yes, the charm of youth....

The Super-Duper Holiday Pinata

For a number of years the sixth-graders in our district were treated to a Spanish program on closed-circuit television featuring Senor Benito Lueras and an assortment of puppets who helped him teach. It was shown each morning for twenty minutes, and the daily TV lessons were reinforced by the classroom teacher. (I learned more Spanish in those few years than in all of my years of high school and college Spanish courses combined), Once a week for forty minutes an attractive, curvacious and bouncy blonde made the rounds in the district for this purpose. The kids loved her, and I didn't mind her coming around, either. When she suggested to the class and me that we do a Spanish holiday song presentation for the holiday program, we immediately agreed.

"Can we sing about a pinata?" Mary Burgeson, a usually quiet girl, bubbled.

"Can we build the pinata?" shouted Terry Trenkler, with much vocal support from Jim Balke and the Johnson twins. I was pleased because these boys were usually "full of the devil," and now their energies were being channeled constructively.

We planned it. Dave Macomb, Gerald Hartung, Jenny Morrice, Ann Harding, and Holger Vogel were going to be on (our very small) stage dancing around the pinata, while the remainder of the class would be in front of, and slightly to the side of it, singing the pinata song. At the conclusion of the song, Holger would hit the pinata with a stick, and the onstage kids would scramble after the candy that fell out.

On the day of the show, the audience settled into their seats, pleased as usual with the show as it progressed. Our number was near the end of the show. The kids sang the pinata song well and the onstage performers did their routine flawlessly to the end of the song. Then Holger swung the stick mightily and hit the pinata squarely in the middle. The audience watched expectantly. The stick broke in half; the pinata appeared intact and unharmed. Holger appeared a bit startled, but trouper that he is, gave a slightly embarrassed, yet winsome smile to the audience, and again swung mightily, and striking the pinata with even more force than before. The reader is reminded that Holger was put together at a time when, and place where, there was no shortage of materials; his determination bordered on awesome. A considerable percentage of the audience winced. The very air seemed to be shattered by the force of Holger's blow, but the stick broke in half again. The audience, though they were sympathetic, couldn't help but laugh a little, much as they tried to squelch it. Now poor Holger looked like a kid who got caught with his hand in the cookie jar.

"Hit it again, Holger," someone shouted.

"Yeah, smack it," squealed someone's grandmother.

Holger swung a third time. The stick broke a third time and Holger was left holding a stub. He turned to the audience wearing the expression of one who couldn't quite believe what had happened, shrugged his shoulders, and exited, stage left. Dave Chase, our backstage boy, wisely closed the curtain. Everyone exploded into uproarious laughter. There was no squelching any laughter now. People were slapping their knees, sliding half off their chairs, etc. Paul Lippold, the principal, Jake Young, a parent, and I were laughing so hard we were near tears. A scene like that, so spontaneous, so unrehearsed, couldn't possibly be programmed better. The three of us then went to find Holger backstage to assure him he was not at fault, that the audience loved him. Holger, good sport that he was, joined in the laughter.

Later, in the classroom, it took half an hour to break the pinata.

"I knew I should've supervised those pinata builders closer," I said, to the class's amusement.

We bounced it, we jumped on it—nothing. Finally, Norm Duncan jumped on it with the heels of his cowboy boots and broke it. That was some pinata!

How to Play Winning Football

The park district in our town had some good programs for the kids. Among these programs were interschool competitions in basketball, flag football, soccer, and softball.

In an effort to persuade the coaches (usually teachers) to give playing time to all the kids who came to play, team standings were not kept for most of the season. Near the end of the season the teams entered into a single-elimination tournament to determine the champion. Pleasant Lane School often did well in this competition.

A flag football game comes to mind. In a quarter-final game we were faced with Green Valley School which, that year, had a talented and quite large team—I don't mean in number; many of their boys were big.

It was a cold, rather wet day. It had rained during the school day, and the footing was not very good. Green Valley scored first. Then we scored. The styles of the teams were quite different from one another. Green Valley used mostly power to move the football. And why not? Their boys were bigger. My boys relied on speed, deception, and excellent play execution. But as the game wore on, it appeared that power was going to win that day. We entered the closing moments of the game behind by a point; we had been unsuccessful in an extra-point attempt. For the last series of plays we ran a single-wing-type play in which the ball is snapped directly to the tailback, who drives off right tackle but hands the ball to another back just behind the line of scrimmage, who then pitches a lateral to the wingback, who has come from the right side and is attempting to circle the left end. The boy who takes the handoff and then pitches to the wingback must be a good ball handler. Our good ball handler was

Craig Cox, a small boy with lots of heart. He shared that backfield spot with Jerry Scharli. Of the two, Scharli was the better runner; he was our best runner. After the play just described, Scharli would replace Cox, and we would run a sweep around right end with a full backfield and a pulling guard in front of the ball carrier.

When the boys lined up for the next play, they seemed hesitant and tentative; they were looking back to the sidelines. Then it dawned on me: Jerry Scharli was not in the backfield!

"Jerry, Jerry," I called. He was standing next to me on my left side.

"Oh, I forgot," he said excitedly.

We had done this several times; I didn't ever send him in. He simply went in. He started to run into the game, but I grabbed his arm and held him back. We would have been penalized for delay of the game.

All we could do is watch as Craig Cox, the wrong player for this maneuver, expertly followed his blockers and scored the winning touchdown! And yes, we did win the flag football championship.

Alengo's Alleycats

While I was teaching during the 1960s at Pleasant Lane School, enrollment was up over most of the country. We had three sections of every grade level, kindergarten through sixth grade, and most of them were large classes. It happened that one grade level, by a coincidence which occasionally occurs, had a predominance of boys. Most of them were not merely boys by name only. They were, what some people call, "all boy." There were many of what educators politely call "management problems." That's a tactful way of saying they were brats. They were as scrappy and rough-and-tumble a group as anyone had witnessed in quite some time. And, of course, with such a predominance in the number of boys, each of the three sections of that grade level had only a smattering of girls.

The spring before this particular grade level became sixth-graders, I approached my principal, Paul Lippold, a fine gentleman, with a simple plan to alleviate this "topheavy with boys" problem in each of the three sixth-grade classrooms.

"Paul, how about giving me an all-boy class, and then the other two classes could have as many girls as boys in them; at least we could have better balance in two of those classrooms."

"You have it," Paul said quickly, afraid I'd change my mind if he hesitated for a split second.

In the days which followed, though Paul and the rest of the staff were delighted, they gently kidded me about having a case of temporary insanity for having volunteered.

But it turned out to be one of the best years I had as a teacher and, I like to believe, one of the best also for many of those boys. My willingness to have them was well publicized, and the feeling quickly became mutual among class members and me. We seemed to understand a great deal about one another—that seemed to be one advantage of an all-male group. We had a good chemistry. This is not to say that they immediately became gentlemen and that we all enjoyed a tranquil year. Hogwash! We had some rocky times, and I dealt out some tongue-lashings, but I tried to be fair (and I believe I was), and rough moments like those were over quickly and forgotten.

We learned in class to recognize and compliment good work. The once wild, garrulous gang, often split by factions, began to achieve a cohesiveness which was, as far as I was concerned, a joy to behold. We all seemed to sense and see it happening before our very eyes, and we all felt grateful for and proud of it.

While we were preparing for a PTA open house that year, a small part of the preparation was to capture the imagination of our people and, as usual, I assigned small committees to create something interesting in various parts of the room and hall for our open house guests. The boys, whose responsibility was to decorate the hall immediately outside the classroom posted silhouettes of cats' heads (made of colored construction paper) on the wall—three rows of them, ten in each row. On each cat's head was posted a small head-photo of a boy in the class, along with his name. Above the three rows was a cat's head with my head-photo and name, plus, in letters larger than the others, the phrase "Top Cat." Above all of this, in yet larger letters, was the heading, "Alengo's Alleycats." It was one of those things which seemed appropriate, considering the makeup of the class and all of the circumstances. After our school won the interschool flag football championship that fall, the local newspaper ran a story and a picture of the players and me (their coach), and referred to us in the story and headline as "Alengo's Alleycats."

A few years later when I became principal, the parents, staff, and student body warmed my heart with a display of affection when, as a surprise at an assembly to recognize the efforts of our honor students, the PTA president proclaimed the official name of the competitive teams "Alleycats, and presented me with a team jersey with the school name and a cartoon of a fierce-looking alleycat's head on the front. I was very touched, and I'll never forget it.

Sally Rand and the Merciful Winners

In 1965, during the time of the all-boy class, we were playing a basketball game in our gym one day against Butterfield School from the southwest corner of town. The park district supplied the schedule and the officials while the schools supplied the gymnasiums, teams, and coaches. Any kid who wanted to could play, so long as he came to practice. It was a good program. Since I had played varsity basketball in high school, I loved the game, its strategies, and other aspects. I was able, in large part, to pass my enthusiasm on to the boys (and girls too), and usually we had a very good team. For one, our transition game was good. We were able, from a zone defense, to form a half-circle with three or four boys around the basket to get the rebound whenever the other team missed a shot. While this was going on, we would, by plan, release one or two boys to scamper upcourt. When we got the rebound off our defensive board, often we could throw the ball the length of the court to whomever we had released. The other teams rarely got back on defense in time. In the event of our opponents hustling back on defense, we had a few basic plays which worked quite well. There were only about three simple plays, each with a couple of options. We could work them from the left or right side of the floor. They worked for two reasons: They were few and simple, and we practiced them quite a bit. But for the opposition (and you must remember these were sixth-graders), considering the options, it caused confusion.

One play which worked very well for us was something I called a "Sally Rand." One of the guards would pass the ball to the forward on his side near the sideline at about the free throw line (as if it extended to the sideline); then the forward from the other side would cut across to the side of the lane to receive a short pass; then the guard from the opposite side would cut down that side of the lane to the basket (we called this maneuver "back door.") and receive a short, usually underhand pass for an easy layup.

When I first introduced this play, the kids asked, "Who's Sally Rand, Mr. A.?"

"Ask your dad at dinner tonight," I advised them.

The next day at practice they were all smiles and giggles as they told me their dads had told them about Sally Rand. While they occasionally botched up other plays, they never forgot how to run a Sally Rand.

We were about midway through the fourth quarter and were beating our opponents rather soundly. I had used all twenty of my players, five in each of four quarters. It was my habit to periodically send a boy who wasn't playing at the moment to the scorer's table to keep me abreast of the score, since we didn't have scoreboards like the high schools. I had sent Johnny Biehl, and he came back and said, "Mr. Alengo, we're ahead twenty-two to nothing."

"Nothing?" I asked. I hadn't realized Butterfield hadn't scored. That bothered me, very much. I called a time out.

"Boys," I began slowly, "I'll probably never ask you to do this again, but please—we can't let these boys go home without a basket. Please don't make it look too obvious, but let them shoot—guard them a little looser—and if they miss, let them get the rebound and shoot again. Fall down—anything, but not too obvious—and let them score, please! To not allow them to score seems to me a form of man's inhumanity to man."

They looked at one another and at me as if they had suddenly, joyously, learned a new concept (which I believe they did). It was as if they had found something valuable they thought they had lost.

"Yeah, Mr. A., good idea," several of them said. We all held hands in our huddle, nodded, and then play resumed.

Sure enough, Butterfield was able to get off a shot, and wonder of wonders, were able to get a couple of rebounds and put the ball in the basket. Actually, they shot three baskets. My players during that time seemed suddenly to find the floor slippery under their feet, and the Butterfield players were none the wiser. But Bob Edwards, their coach, was. He quickly came over to us after the game, shook my hand, thanked me, and gave me a knowing wink.

Later at home when I told my wife Elaine, a primary grades teacher, how we had almost shut out the other team before I became aware of it, she gave me her "my husband is a big dummy" expression, but she was glad we finally allowed the other team to score.

Some Classroom Thoughts at Large

The following are bits of wisdom and considerations that have helped from time to time.

1. Why do we call it a "hot water heater"? Why would you heat hot water?
2. "Past experience"—is there any other?
3. "Shorter hours"—I've always thought sixty minutes was too long.
4. You don't have to be an athlete to be a sport.
5. You don't have to be a farmer to be outstanding in your field.
6. People called me "P.J.," but my son called me "Collect."
7. You can call me anything, but don't call me late for dinner.
8. Two wrongs don't make a right.
9. The harder I work, the luckier I get.
10. Promising is good, but performing is better.
11. It takes two to tangle.
12. Speak softly and carry a big smile.
13. It is better to be a has-been than a never-been.
14. Ideas don't work unless you do.
15. The difference between champ and chump is "u."
16. Hindsight is better than foresight.
17. Monday morning quarterbacks never lose a game.
18. It is better to remain silent and be thought a fool than to speak up and remove all doubt.
19. Give a man a fish and feed him for a day; teach him to fish and feed him for a lifetime.
20. The older I get, the smarter my parents become.

The Gunfighter

The time came when I became the principal of Pleasant Lane School. Most people think of school principals as rather serious people, dedicated to their work, schools, students, staff, and the like. This is largely true, there is certainly dedication to the work and such involvement.

I confess, however, that we principals have our moments. When you consider the fact that most principals were once classroom teachers, and you consider that classroom teachers spend much of their time trapped with young people, you can see how it helps considerably for each teacher to have a sense of humor, which most of them do. The logical thinking is that most of the newly promoted principals would retain the sense of humor. This, also, is largely true, regardless of the fact that many mask it with a serious facial expression and manner.

In my experience, this mask often comes off when principals are together or away from the public.

One day when I had business at the board of education office, I thought I spotted my old pal Joe Koutny, another principal in the district, standing with his back to me. He seemed to be discussing some school business with Sylvia Whitton, secretary in that office.

I stepped into the doorway and in a loud voice declared, "This town isn't big enough for both of us, Joe Koutny. Turn around and face your death." I stood ready with my imaginary six-shooter, ready to fire a volley of shots into him.

He turned around. It wasn't Joe Koutny. It was Ted Arenberg, president of the board of education.

I stared unbelievingly at him and said, "Why, you're not Joe Koutny." (brilliant, huh?)

But I could see he had a twinkle in his eye, so I pressed my luck, "Why are you going around looking like Joe? Don't you know that's dangerous? I almost shot you."

"I'm terribly sorry," he said, getting into character. "I'll try not to do it again." He was smiling now.

Meanwhile Sylvia was howling with laughter, and went into an absolute peal. Still laughing, her business with Arenberg finished, she excused herself to take a break.

"I've got to tell the other girls," she gushed. Somehow I knew my notoriety was getting a fresh start that day.

School Phobia

One day I received a phone call from the principal of a parochial school in our town. She advised me that we were going to be enrolling Shirley Lemak (not her real name) shortly. She explained that Shirley was an incorrigible truant and that, in truth, they were relieved to be rid of her. The parents, she added, could do nothing, as Shirley defied their efforts to get her to school.

I suspected a deep-seated psychological problem and notified our social worker, Kathleen Fitzgerald, a real crackerjack professional. Beside being a terrific social worker, she is also one of the world's finest human beings. She easily gains the confidence of most people because she talks so well. I don't mean she sounds politically or socially correct, or any other trendy thing. Rather, she sounds like your friend next door who is very sympathetic. But she's also very knowledgeable without being intimidating. Having six kids of her own adds to her credibility.

Together we drew up a plan for a team effort which included the parents and a county psychiatrist. The parents were quite distraught, understandably. They had gone through hell with their daughter's school phobia at the other school, and they were certain it would continue at our school.

The plan was for Shirley's mom and a neighbor to bring Shirley to school shortly after the other children had come into the building. That way, if there was any scene, most of the children wouldn't see it.

There were many scenes. "I won't go," Shirley would say. Several times I had to go to the car and dislodge Shirley because her resolve was so strong that her mom and the neighbor couldn't handle her.

"Don't touch me!" she'd scream.

I would tuck her under my arm like a football and hang on tight, with her hitting me with her fists and screaming all the while, then deposit her on the threshold of her classroom. Strangely, once she was over the threshold, she was okay. It was one of the darnedest things I'd ever seen.

We kept doing this until she gave it up. It took approximately four months. Then Shirley came to school willingly and lined up with the other children, exactly as the psychiatrist had predicted. Meanwhile, the social worker, Kathleen and I met several times with her mom and dad. They had witnessed the change in their daughter, and now actually saw her wanting to learn and attend school.

"We're so grateful. You've done the impossible," they said. They thought it was nothing short of a miracle, and held us high in their esteem. "Do you walk on water?" they asked after their daughter seemed to have made a full recovery.

"We'd like to have you come to our house for dinner," Kathleen and I usually try to sidestep these invitations, but it was so sincere that we accepted.

Shirley went through the rest of elementary, junior high and high school without incident, and graduated in the upper one-fourth of her class.

We saw Shirley's parents a number of times before I retired, and they always told us enthusiastically that she had grown up a well-adjusted girl.

Kute Kindergartners

If there's anyone other than a Marilyn Monroe who has taken my breath away, it's a kindergarten kid—not in the same way, of course, but they are delightful just the same. Kindergartners knock me out. Sometimes they say and do the darndest things out of the most absolute innocence, and in those moments they are without peers as charmers and comics.

During my tenure as a principal, I visited classes often to keep abreast of how the kids were progressing, and to keep tabs on the teaching staff, too. Sometimes, by plan, I taught a lesson in social studies, language arts, or math, just to keep my hand in it. The teachers appreciated it, and the kids seemed to like it, too.

Of all the kids, kindergartners were, perhaps, my favorite. One time when I was walking in the hall, I smiled at a mother and her kindergarten boy whom she had come to pick up at the end of his session. Unaware that her boy knew me well from my visits, she asked him if he knew who I was.

"Oh, sure, I know him by heart," he assured her.

Another tale has one of our kindergarten teachers, Marge McMullen, trying to elicit responses from a painfully shy Suzie the first day of school, with no success. Several additional tries brought the same result. If she could only get Suzie to open up a little, Marge would help her. Marge saw her best chance during a break, when Suzie was looking with obvious interest at a bulletin board featuring Little Bo Peep. Marge came quietly to Suzie and gently asked her if she had a good summer.

"Yes," came Suzie's short reply.

This was not easy. Still Marge, undaunted, carried on. "Do you like the bulletin board?"

"Yes," the non-talkative Suzie again replied.

Marge decided to stay with it. Maybe she could get her to relax and talk about the bulletin board which had captured her attention.

"Do you know who that is?" she asked, pointing to Bo Peep.

"No."

"If I give you a hint, will you try to guess?"

"Yesss," said Suzie more slowly, breaking into a smile.

Now we were getting somewhere, Marge thought.

"Her name is Bo...." said Marge, who smiled and tilted her ear toward Suzie.

"Bo Derrick!" said Suzie triumphantly.

Another time, before the start of school in September, our kindergarten teacher, with parental help, was doing kindergarten screening to help determine which youngsters were prepared to enter kindergarten. The screening consisted of a series of simple tasks which each child was asked to perform.

Meanwhile, I had a message in the office for one of the parents in the kindergarten room, and I briskly walked down the hall and had turned to enter through the doorway when Ronnie Grove, a newly enrolled kindergartner, closed the door in my face. I mean, I darn near broke my nose on that door. I was surprised and bewildered. Ronnie looked up at me with an expression that seemed to say that he was not to blame — that he had done as he had been told. A glance at the teacher and her parent-helpers revealed them covering their laughing faces with their hands. It seems that as part of the screening, Ronnie was asked to close the door. Then along came this principal, and....

But Ronnie was like that. For the next seven years Ronnie did exactly as he was asked, but none of it was so memorable as that time.

Telephone Excitement

When I returned from a principals' meeting late one morning, I looked at a few notes scattered on my desk that had been put there by the secretary, and saw that there was one written by a teacher.

Mary Weck, who had written a name and phone number only on her note, was the teacher. She was a very good special education teacher who did wonders with kids with learning disabilities. A bright and expressive person, she usually did not have such economy with words, so I went to her to see if I could get an idea of what the woman wanted.

She explained to me, rather hurriedly because she was busy, that the woman wanted to enroll her child in our school, but Mary wasn't sure if they lived in our school attendance area.

I returned to my office, dialed the number, and was astonished when I reached the party at the other end.

"Hello, big boy. My name is Bambi, and I can show you a real good time, better than you've ever had. I will awaken your senses like you can never imagine; you will thrill to my touch!" The message continued in one of the sexiest voices I've ever heard.

I'm sure I blushed, even though I was alone. I felt my cheeks grow hot. Then I came back to reality and couldn't help but chuckle.

When my lunch break came, I went to the teacher's room where I knew I'd find Mary. I recognized by her expression and the twinkle in her eye that she knew I had made the call. She broke into a giggle, and so did I.

"That was a good one, Mary," I told her. "Now I owe you one, and you'll never know when I'll strike."

After having a cup of coffee with her and returning to my office, I thought, I'll bet I can get Burckle to bite on this, so I called Bob Burckle, who was the principal of a school whose attendance area was one of those adjacent to mine.

"Bob, I got a call from this woman who wants to enroll her child in school. They just moved here over the weekend. I'm sure they live in your attendance area. Give her a call, will you?"

"Sure thing. I'll get right on it," he said.

Ten minutes later my phone rang. When I picked it up, I recognized his laughter.

"You spaghetti-bending rascal," he said (I'm of Italian descent). I never dreamed about who'd be at the other end of my phone call. I'm calling Bob Nelson at Butterfield School to get him to bite the same as I did. See you later."

"The devil made me do it," I laughed.

A couple of hours later, around a quarter of four my phone rang, and when I picked it up, Joe Koutny, principal of Lincoln School, another school whose attendance area was adjacent to mine, was on the line.

"Joe," he began, "a woman who recently moved in, called me about registering her boy in school, but I think she's in your attendance area. Will you give her a call?"

I laughed the laugh that told him I knew what he was up to.

"Joe, that bogus phone call must have gone around the entire district. Geez, I hope the public doesn't find out about it."

I went to Mary, and told her that the message she had left me had made its way around the entire district. We had a good laugh again.

"But be careful who you tell about it," I told her. "It could cause a public relations explosion."

We were all cautious, and nothing more came of it.

The New Phenom

This is a story I have to credit to Dr. Ralph Belnap of Northern Illinois University. A few years ago, he told it at a convention of the Illinois Principals Association.

A school district had hired a young, new sixth-grade teacher whose credentials were good, and he seemed to be quite bright and alert on his feet.

The first time his principal visited his classroom to observe, he immediately noticed that all the kids seemed enthusiastic. In addition, they all—all—looked excited, and they all—all—had their hands raised, indicating they knew the answers. Even the kids who were thought to be slow learners, with low IQs, who hadn't done a lick of work in years...they all had their hands raised!

The principal hurried to tell the curriculum director about the new phenom.

"He's terrific," he told her. She visited with the same result. Soon the word spread to the assistant superintendent. "He's terrific," she told him. Then the word spread to the superintendent. "He's terrific," he was told. Then the word spread to the president of the board of education. "He's terrific."

All the kids had their hands raised, eagerly to answer questions. When the visits came unannounced, it made no difference.

"We've got ourselves some kind of a boy, here," declared the superintendent.

Everyone agreed. "What a phenom," they said.

In a relatively short time, the newly discovered phenom quickly rose in the ranks up the ladder. When he became the boss of the principal who had first seen him, he was asked, "How'd you do it? Every kid—every kid, even the lazy ones, even the slow ones—every kid had his hand up to answer your questions, some of the questions that might be tough for a college kid to answer. Did they all really know the answers?"

"Good grief, no," answered the phenom.

"Well, how then?"

"On the first day of school," began the phenom, "I said to the class, 'if someone walks into this room, raise your hand to any question I ask. If you know the answer, raise your right hand. If you don't, raise your left.'"

Who Wudda Thunk It?

    Sometimes the darnedest things happen. You can't predict them because they're so bizaare, like the time one of our fourth-grade classes was coming in from the playground after recess. The teachers usually have their groups stop outside the door before entering the building to get them settled and quiet for their walk through the hall back to their classrooms. In this case, the teacher was talking to a boy near the back of the line when a shoving match broke out near the front. Recognizing that the shoving might escalate to something more dangerous, she told the boy to wait there while she broke up the shoving match. After she had done so, she forgot about the boy near the end of the line and brought her group back to the classroom. He, however, having been told to wait there, stayed there. Meanwhile, it began to rain hard. Our boy stayed on his spot, then finally went home when the dismissal bell for lunch sounded. My office phone rang. Our boy's mother was at the other end, and she gave me hell! When you hear the expression that someone doesn't have sense to come in out of the rain, be prepared to believe it.

    Then I had an experience with a fourth grade boy who was misbehaving a lot, for four consecutive school days. When his teacher understandably brought him to me to see what I could do, I thought it would be a good idea to have the boy telephone his mother from my office phone and explain to her, in my presence, exactly why he was calling, and also explain his exact misbehavior. The moment his mother answered the phone at her end, the boy launched into a crying marathon. When he regained his composure, he explained the reason for the call, and about his four consecutive days of misbehavior. When I was satisfied that he had done his part, I talked for a few minutes with his mother, who apologized for his misbehavior and promised that she and her husband would straighten the kid out.

The next day I received a phone call from the boy's father, who angrily told me that because the boy was crying when his mother answered the phone, she had pictured him beaten up and bloody in a ditch somewhere, and that I had used poor judgment. I acknowledged that I now understood how the maneuver could backfire, and that I was sorry for it, even though it seemed like a good idea at the time. You never know.

In another instance, a fifth-grade girl came running up to me on the playground during the lunch hour speechless. The reason she couldn't talk—a popsicle she had purchased from the ice cream man was stuck to her tongue. I brought her into the nurse's office and poured a glass of water on it until it became unglued.

When I returned to the playground, a parent supervisor who had seen what had happened said, "I'll bet that's the craziest thing you've seen happen around here."

"Would you like to hear of another one from last year?" I asked.

"Yes, I would."

I told her that one day a year ago I was interviewing a prospect for our primary grades. My answer to a knock on my office door revealed a teacher with a first-grade boy who somehow managed to hang a chair around his neck. His head was too large to remove the chair. We freed him by sawing off a slat of the back support.

This was a good kid. Anyway, how can you become angry with a first-grader?

The primary prospect I had been interviewing, thought the event was hilarious and that the boy was "precious." I hired her on the spot.

The Apple Polisher

Julius Caesar, his murderers claimed, was slain because of his ambition. For whatever reason, it caused quite an upset and led to more bloodshed in the ensuing battle for revenge.

These days people usually aren't murdered for being ambitious or for allied reasons such as apple polishing, but in my experience, the urge to kill apple-polishers still beats within the human heart. The consequences of breaking the law against this these days are, perhaps, the only reason some of these people are spared from their resentful colleagues.

Principal John Bucholtz (not his real name) was at once the most blatant and at times skillful apple-polisher I've ever known. He cultivated friendships with whomever was important at the moment, be they board of education members, superintendents, or some important parents or citizens. John, I believe, would never be out of a job. He patronized too many important people for that to even have been a possibility.

The other side of the coin is that he would not give you a glimmer of recognition if you were not important in some way. Rumor had it that he treated some of his teachers badly. Some, however, who were in favor with the administration, board members, or important parents were treated well by him. That's the way he was. Indeed, I could gauge my own status with the administration and board by the way John treated me. If he patronized me, I knew my star shone brightly with our local organizational power structure. If he shunned me, it was probably strong evidence that my status with the important people was low. Some resentful group members thought he brightened a room whenever he exited.

John seemed to spend a lot of time away from his building.

It was said he spent much time at the board office. He seemed always to know what was going on, or what, of any importance, was about to happen in the district. He issued invitations of one kind or another to some important people. He seemed to be the consummate politician. The trouble was, he was all for John Bucholtz. Many sincerely believed he didn't care a snap of his fingers about most of the kids enrolled in his school, nor the teaching staff, except in circumstances where he saw that they might be helpful to him. Yet, in truth, he didn't do a bad job. Many things turned out right coincidentally, in spite of his apple-polishing.

Some people wouldn't put anything past him. One day my friend, whom I will call Harry, who was another principal in town, went to John's office, inasmuch as they were a committee of two who were assigned a small task by the superintendent. When Harry arrived, John was elsewhere in the building, but the secretary invited him to go into his office, saying John would be there shortly. John had carelessly left a copy of Harry's goals on the desk top. By way of explanation, each principal was to write a set of professional goals for himself and his school each year. The original went to the superintendent, and each principal kept a copy of his own. These were of a confidential nature. Yet here was a copy of Harry's goals in John's hands. How did he get them? Why? Of what value would they be? The only apparent thing was that John somehow had gotten a key to Harry's office, snuck in, and stolen a copy. Maybe John had a copy of all the principals' goals. Knowing him, he probably saw some advantage, real or imagined, in having them.

Harry was furious. He asked John, when he returned, what he was doing with his goals. Caught by surprise, having forgotten to place the goals in a drawer out of sight, John was unable to explain it to Harry's satisfaction, and finally offered as a response, "I can't tell you now."

"Baloney," shot back Harry. "You're a sneaky SOB, and I don't want anything to do with you!" With that, he turned on his heel and walked out.

I don't know how John excused himself, but I know he talked to the superintendent about it shortly thereafter and came out okay. Sometimes I wonder if there's any real justice in the world.

Sometimes You Just Can't Win

Ever hear of the Slossen IQ test? It's a quick, individual oral test which can be given by a principal or teacher so that you can get a rough idea, say, of how a new student is able to perform. Oftentimes this information is otherwise delayed while you wait for the new student's records to arrive from his last school. Getting an idea of his capabilities helps you to serve him better, more meaningfully. This is merely one use for the test. There is more than one way it can be useful.

Usually IQ tests are given in large groups, an entire class at a time, and usually they take a rather long time. These are given by the classroom teacher. Sometimes, if a student is being considered for Special Education, a psychologist gives a battery of tests (individually), one of which is an IQ test. The chances for accuracy are probably best in this situation, but that is not to say that a group-IQ or Slossen quick-individual test is not reliable because results have proven otherwise. I'm merely saying that the one the psychologist gives is considered the "best of the best."

Our assistant superintendent of instruction purchased a Slossen for use by each of the principals one year after we had discussed its advantages at length.

One day a few years later, one of our teachers was having a conference with the mother of one of her fifth-grade boys. Because he was a transfer student from outside the district and we didn't have anything official in the way of results from a test of his ability to think and to learn, the teacher routinely asked the boy's mother for permission to have the principal give the Slossen IQ, explaining that it was only an informal, one-on-one kind of a thing, and it might give us something to consider along with his classroom performance. There was no problem.

I administered the Slossen test early the next morning. It took about fifteen minutes.

Later that morning, another administrator, whom I'll call Dan, came storming into my office with the sudden surprise of a gas main explosion. He was quite upset. At first I didn't know why. He had been an administrator and outside of the classroom for quite a long time. Much of what went on in schools in the meantime had passed him by.

"For Christ's sake, what're you doing, Joe?" he demanded.

"What do you mean?" I asked.

"Dammit, Joe, I want to know what's going on!" he shouted.

"Well, dammit, Dan, so do I. I know you didn't come just to show your pretty face." (Dan's face, though usually smiling, resembled that of a retired pug who had taken too many punches to the head.)

It turned out they'd received a phone call at the board office from a hysterical woman who was so upset she couldn't make herself understood due to her combination of crying, shouting, sobbing, and the like. Finally she was able to communicate that she had agreed to the Slossen test but had changed her mind and didn't want it administered. I don't know why she didn't call us.

If Dan had been alert and on top of things in education, he might have calmed her down and reassured her that it was only a routine thing which was done all the time; in fact many schools didn't even ask parental permission, as we did. This woman had some strange idea that this test was some kind of dangerous, voodoo thing. Incredible as it might seem, people occasionally think these things. Also, if Dan had been on top of things, he would have realized the Slossen test is purposely designed to be given by a principal or teacher. But Dan was not on top of things. He shielded himself from the everyday grass roots of education and had only a vague notion of what went on. He thought only psychologists were permitted to give any IQ tests, even though classroom teachers had been giving group-type IQ tests for as long as I can remember, and even though he was physically present at the administrative meeting when the decision was made to purchase the Slossen IQ tests for use by principals and teachers in individual cases.

The fact that I'd already given the Slossen test to the woman's son made Dan furious.

"Why didn't you ask our permission?" he demanded.

"Why don't you wake up and smell the coffee!" I shouted back in reply. "You hired me to run this place, and I'm doing it. Find out the facts before you open your big mouth. I did what we're supposed to do. If you didn't crumble from the pressure of one lousy phone call, we'd be okay. If you can't stand the heat, get the hell out of the kitchen," I paraphrased. "We get phone calls every day. We deal with them. Can't you handle it? These Slossens are designed to be given by principals or teachers, Dan. That's why we got them!"

I couldn't dissuade him from going down the hall to see Georgia Lange, the teacher, where he interrupted her class, requesting that she come into the hall to ask her the obvious: Had the mother agreed to the Slossen test the previous day? Of course, the mother had, and when Georgia learned of the woman's frantic phone call and Dan's reaction to it, she was very upset.

Dan insisted I phone the woman and offer to not post the Slossen test results in the boy's school record. "Okay," I said. "Now, if you'll kindly get lost, I've got work to do." He left, and I never heard another word from him about it.

Dan Scores Again

For a number of years at Pleasant Lane School I had been trying to have a roomful of old wooden first-grade desks replaced with formica-top desks. I met with absolutely no success. My reasoning was that the old (very old) desks had bruises, grooves, ridges, etc., and it was difficult for the kids to write.

Our business manager, Cal Defenbau, was the thriftiest human being I'd ever met (some called him cheap). He simply found it very difficult to part with a dollar. The taxpayers didn't really realize what a tax-saving friend they had in Cal. I liked him personally because I believed he was trying earnestly to save dollars, but his frugality sometimes drove me near to distraction. So the desks with decent tops for first grade were put on hold indefinitely.

One cold February day, moments after the kids were dismissed from school at the end of the day, I was informally conferencing with a member of my teaching staff in my office with the door open when Dan charged in and started berating me as if no one was there except me.

"Jesus Christ, Joe, why haven't you replaced those old first-grade desks? They're really in sad shape—all grooved up—and they must be a hundred years old. How could you let that happen? I was just in there with a board member, and we were looking at some buildings, and he saw them. It's embarrassing, Joe!"

With that, he turned and walked out. The teacher and I were flabbergasted. I stood with my mouth open for some seconds. Then I remembered how hard I had tried to have them replaced, and I became angry.

"We'll continue this later," I told the teacher. She knew I had tried to replace the desks, and understood. Then I ran after

Dan. He was twenty feet from the outside door when I reached him. I matched him stride for stride as I gave him some of the best hell I could muster.

"You big-mouth ignoramous," I began. "Do you know how long I've been trying to have those desks replaced? Do you know what's going on in this district, or do you deliberately try to create foolish situations? Dan, I've been trying for years to get new desktops for that room! Do you ever check these things out?" I went on and on.

Suddenly I felt very, very cold—practically numbing. I was shivering. It didn't take long to figure it out. In my passionate anger, I had walked out the front door with Dan as he was walking to his car, all the while I was giving him hell. It was eleven degrees above zero, and I was in my shirtsleeves.

I stopped, suddenly realizing my situation, and said, "You can stay out here all day, Dan, but I'm cold. I'm going back in. Nuts to you!"

As I headed back into the building, I could hear Dan laughing as he walked the rest of the distance to his car.

Lover Boy

When my wife and I and our two children came to live in our town, we had the good fortune to enter into a strong friendship with Carol and Bill Smith and their three children. They were very kind to us. Socially, they included us in their circle; through them we met and became friends with many other fine people. They probably didn't need to be so nice to us, because they were as handsome a couple as can be imagined. Bill was classically handsome, had all of his hair and a quick wit, while Carol was gorgeous as can be and seemed not to realize it. Being a few years older than my wife and I, their children were a few years older than ours as well; one of them often babysat for our two, and did a fine job. Our kids loved her.

Carol, as it happened, worked as a secretary at the board of education office, and usually answered the phone there. One day when I had some routine business with an assistant superintendent who worked closely with school principals, I rang up the board office. That day everything up to that point had gone right for me, and I felt good. When the phone was picked up at the other end, I breezily said, "Hello, Carol, sweetheart. This is Joe. How are you?"

"This is Virginia Huckstedt," came the hesitant reply.

"Uh, oh, er—Hello, Virginia, sweetheart, how are you?" I tried to recover, but my voice sounded like something between a gasp and a death rattle.

Now I could hear Virginia giggling. Then she said, "Carol's on a break, and I'm covering her phone, but I'll get your sweetheart." I heard more giggling.

"No, that's okay, Virginia; I'll call later."

At this moment, I regret having written this book as a first-person narrative because at times like this, one exhibits oneself as a damn fool.

In another incident during some of my tenure at Pleasant Lane School, before I was transferred to another school in the district, I had as efficient and attractive a secretary as I ever have had. She had come to us when our secretary of some years relocated to St. Louis. I had phoned Geri Wilson (not her real name), secretary at another school, to get the phone number of a friend of hers who was reportedly between jobs, only to learn that Geri was interested in our position, and her friend had already filled another secretarial position. I learned from the superintendent's secretary that there was "one of those things"—a personality conflict between Geri and her principal, an attractive woman herself—which it seemed couldn't be resolved.

I had taken problem-people from other schools before, usually with considerable success, and we did need a secretary. I had a gut feeling she was okay and would fit in.

I was wrong. She wasn't okay. She was better. She was excellent. She was cheerful and pleasant to the staff and the public, and her phone work was fine. Doing paperwork—a breeze. And so was taking care of all the intangibles. She seemed able to adjust to my every move, and to those of the entire school.

We worked very well together, and in the process, became good friends. After three years, as I said, I was transferred to Green Valley, another school in the district, and Geri's old boss came to Pleasant Lane. Good-bye, Geri. She was out of a job for a while. Some months later, when Green Valley's secretary was out for a few weeks for surgery, Geri filled in quite capably for us.

Then Geri caught as a secretary in a business nearby. It was during this time that she began having trouble at home which eventually ended in divorce. Meanwhile, we were still good friends and confidants. We lunched together at a number of out-of-the-way places, and I consoled and advised her as best I could about her circumstances. We told no one of our meetings because we simply thought it best not to. I have many friends who are women and have lunch with them with no hesitation. So long as the women are matronly, or older, or whatever, that's okay. But if a woman is as attractive as Geri, and you're seen with her shortly before she divorces her husband look out—that's dynamite!

One day while Geri and I were having lunch at what we thought was an out-of-the-way place, two administrators from a nearby district walked in. They knew us. Geri wisely advised me that we should stay. "After all, lots of people have lunch together," she said. "It'll look suspicious if we leave abruptly." And of course she was right. But I blew it.

"Let's leave," I insisted. "Maybe they haven't seen us." I forced the issue, and we left hurriedly out the back way.

They had seen us, and as Geri had predicted, our leaving out the back way looked very suspicious. Before you could say "I'm innocent," rumors that we were having an affair were being whispered. Some good friends of mine quietly and secretively asked me, and I denied it. I said things, like "That sounds absolutely fascinating," and, "It just isn't true." They didn't believe me. They seemed to look at me with—what, a new respect, a new fascination?—as if I had a mystique about me, a dangerous charm to cause to flutter and to conquer feminine hearts.

I believe some men would gladly admit to having an affair with Geri, maybe even falsify one, but here I was quietly denying it. Truly, I didn't find the idea all that displeasing. I must admit, a small part of me enjoyed it, and at times even felt a bit smug about my new alleged reputation as a lover.

Some Dark and Bright Hours

When I was transferred to Green Valley School, I found a large segment of the parent group angry at my predecessor for what they claimed was poor discipline and supervision in the school. In my most objective scrutiny, I found it to be representative of most other reasonably run schools in my experience. It appeared to parallel, for instance, the discipline and supervision at Pleasant Lane, my former school, which the parent community and staff there considered to be quite good. Different locations, different personalities, different thinking, but, as I said, this particular parent group at Green Valley saw it as unacceptable.

After a while I learned that it wasn't the discipline and supervision after all, but a personality conflict with the principal before me. In short, a small but influential segment of the parent group simply didn't like him. I'm not sure why, but I'm sure they used the discipline-and-supervision thing as something that sounded more like a legitimate reason to discredit him. I had had considerable success with the parent community at Pleasant Lane, so my boss, Superintendent Bob Chelseth, had made what could be considered a wise move in sending me to Green Valley to see what I could do there.

In order to save face, this parent group still claimed that there was a discipline and supervision problem upon my arrival, but I reasoned it would fade away with the passage of time. However, to borrow a line from Shakespeare, I was to suffer the slings and arrows of outrageous fortune myself: In October, a tough kid from Chicago's inner city enrolled, and in November he willfully and deliberately slammed an exit door, repeatedly, on another boy's arm until it broke at the wrist near the heel of the hand. The victim of this assault was one of the most unpopular boys in school. There was good reason for his unpopularity. He was a dishonest, sneaky, sniveling, whining kid who did his best to bait other kids and, you guessed it, the other kids would get into hot water with their teachers. After a while the staff became aware of his motives and practices, but they rarely saw him doing his dirty work. They were obliged to protect him from the outrage of the other children when they were all in our care. I was at a meeting away from the building when it happened at recess late in the morning, away from the supervising teacher, of course. He showed his hand to the teacher and didn't say a word about the door being closed on it. It looked red, nothing too unusual, and he had cried "wolf" so often that the teacher was not alarmed. The student was also a "mama's boy." The teacher sent him to the office for the secretary to look at it, and she assumed the same thing. He was advised to go home for lunch, since the bell was going to ring in a few seconds, and show it to his mother.

About two o'clock that day my office phone rang, and on the line a woman was shouting hysterically and unintelligibly. After some minutes she calmed herself momentarily and told me that her son's wrist had been broken deliberately in a door-closing incident, and that it happened because of our lousy supervision, and so forth, and then the fury was on her again. She was an influential member of the group which liked to run things, so I knew I was in for a siege.

She came at me with a frontal attack at a PTA board meeting, having mobilized her forces beforehand. It was complete with a letter with several copies, and it came up again at the next board of education meeting. It was about poor discipline and supervision at Green Valley School.

I decided to mobilize my staff and, with them, draw up a plan for good supervision and discipline and implement it. We shared the plan at an open PTA meeting and asked for parental help in its implementation. Having been a speech major in my undergrad college days, I mustered up the best, most sincere manner of presentation to an audience of which I was capable. I spoke of our plan, which was outlined in such a way as to have an excellent chance for success—with everyone's cooperation. I spoke sincerely of having faith in the plan, of building on our strengths, and of expecting its successful conclusion.

With the help of a very good teaching staff, we conscientiously put the plan into operation, and it succeeded admirably. The parent group was stripped of that complaint simply because it was obvious to any observer that the discipline and supervision had improved, without question. Thus we had turned a bad situation around inside of a year. We won over the entire parent community, and I could see a school spirit developing within that parent group. All in all, it was very rewarding.

As an addendum to the story, we (and I personally) received an unsolicited "thank you" from the mother whose boy's wrist was broken in the door. She had been so furious that she had immediately withdrawn the boy and his sister from our school and had tried to enroll them in a nearby parochial school. But the boy was listed as having a learning disability two years previously, curiously enough, at the prodding and insistence of the mother who refused to believe he performed poorly because of a lackadaisical attitude toward school work. At her insistence, the school district psychologist had him tested and, owing largely to a lackadaisical attitude toward the test, he performed poorly on that, too, and with the psychologist bending to the mother's will at the time, he was declared borderline eligible for learning disabilities service. His mom had a peculiar notion that, because of the individual attention the kids with learning disability get, her son would have an advantage. But she failed to consider his lackadaisical attitude as a major factor in his poor performance. He progressed as he always had.

His status as a student with a learning disability was standing in his way of his being accepted into the parochial school his mother had chosen. Many parochial schools do not have learning disabilities services, as was the case in this instance. Was it poetic justice?

The boy was accepted, and that principal advised the boy's mother that he had been accepted on my word only. It was at that time that she thanked me.

A Visit From a Real TV Weatherman

One year we arranged for Harry Volkman, a favorite television weatherman in the Chicago area, to come to our school to talk to our fourth, fifth, and sixth grades. One of the reasons for his popularity was that he visited many schools in the area for free, and he had a winning personality. The kids loved him. It had become a tradition for whichever school he visited to present him with a flower corsage which he would wear that same evening on television during his weatherman slot, and he would mention the name of school who gave it to him, and make a fuss over it and the fine youngsters, along with their teachers and principal (a good public relations tactic).

The date was set for the middle of January. There had been two huge snowstorms the week before he came, and snow was everywhere. The streets were plowed and passable, but the snow was piled high, and the temperature was near zero.

After his presentation I took him to a fine local restaurant for lunch, paid for by our PTA. He was immediately recognized by half a dozen patrons who shouted across the room things like, "Hiya, Harry, I watch you all the time on television," and "When you gonna get rid of this snow, Harry?" and so on.

Harry was wonderful. He acknowledged everyone by waving and promising to do his best to get rid of the snow. The waitress was at first so nervous with his celebrity that she could hardly hold her pencil to take our lunch orders, but he put her at ease by asking her if this was her job while working her way through school (she was considerably older than school age), and asking her if there were any lunch specials. The man's charm seemed limitless.

Harry was scheduled to make an appearance in the afternoon at another school in a nearby town, and he had asked me before we left for lunch to have our secretary call them to get instructions on how to get there from our school. Euneece, our secretary, telephoned ahead and wrote the instructions for him, and after lunch, Harry bid me thanks and good-bye, and off he went for his afternoon assignment. When I returned, Euneece told me that when she had phoned the other school for directions for Harry, the secretary there had asked, "He's coming today? Oh my gosh, we thought he was coming on this date next year! We don't have a flower corsage for him. Whatever will we do?"

That same night Elaine and I watched Harry on CBS television. He mentioned both schools and the corsages. My wife walked up close to the TV screen as if her eyesight were faulty. I remember she was squinting. Finally she said, "That corsage from the other school looks like it's made of art construction paper."

"It very well could be," I answered. Then I told her of Euneece's phone call there.

My Beautiful Balloon

My kids, David and Cynthia, were born slightly less than eleven months apart. I took quite a lot of good-natured kidding for that, things like "Irish twins?" and "Did you find out what's causing these children?"

But the closeness in age turned out to be a blessing. They shared many things in common because of it, and on vacations, each had the other as a friend.

Okay, so they weren't always perfect. Maybe they fought some. All right, sometimes they were impossible. Covered in the category of impossible is how they fought at ages two through five when each, for example, was given a matchbox car, but of different colors. Their chief source of gifts, their grandparents, soon learned that they had to be given the exact same thing—same color, same everything!

One Sunday, my mother and father came for dinner and entered the living room with two identical "people" balloons, the kind with the cardboard feet. Each stood about three feet tall. My mother inadvertently backed the one she was holding into a sharp corner of a piece of furniture, and the identical balloon she was holding burst and broke with a loud bang. Without missing a beat David said, "Oh look, Cindy's balloon broke."

We all laughed, and my dad hurried out the door and soon returned with another identical balloon to save the day. We should have figured that Dave was smart, even at that tender age, because of his quick wit, but we didn't realize it until years later.

A Spectator to a Game and Then Some

When my son Dave was a fourth-grader, he coaxed me to attend a father-and-son night at his school with him. I agreed without much coaxing. I like to do things with my kids, and a father-and-son night promised something of masculine interest, usually much better than some old biddy talking about flower arranging or why Johnny can't read (I've heard that one a few times).

Bobby Weiss, a player for the Chicago Bulls at the time, was the speaker, and he was good. He also had some film clips of some Bulls games and a movie regarding the history of pro basketball. As a bonus, I had the winning number for two free tickets to a Bulls game to be held in the near future. These numbers had been given to each member of the audience as we stood in line before entering the meeting.

"Hey, P.J.," I heard as someone tapped me from behind on my right shoulder.

I turned around to my right side, from the direction the shoulder tap had come. There was no one there. When I faced front again I found that Bob Dunne and his boy, our neighbors, had snuck in front of us when we were at the end of the line. They both were giggling at the result of their little joke. It was of no consequence at the time, just their little joke. But it backfired on them: Had they taken their proper place in line behind us, they would have won the free tickets. We all laughed good-naturedly about it.

Dave and I arrived at the Bulls game early. Soon the stadium became crowded. We happened to see a few people we knew, and I called them to draw their attention. We talked with them for a few minutes. Then, moments before the game was to begin, I spotted a friend and work colleague, Herb Elderton (not his real name), and was about to call to him when I suddenly realized the woman with him was not his wife. She was gorgeous—blond, blue-eyed with a trim figure enhanced by a beige knit dress. They sat five rows directly in front of us. Though they behaved in good taste—no necking or kissing—the attention they paid to each other, and the manner in which each looked at and touched the other clearly indicated that they were more than friends.

Herb was a good-looking guy whose manner was usually low-key. It had been whispered that he was unfaithful to his wife, but I liked him and had refused to believe it. Now there was no mistaking it.

My son Dave knew Herb as our families had shared several visits, grilling hamburgers, and the like. I was hoping Dave wouldn't spot Herb because Dave would probably call to him or mention at home the beautiful stranger he had escorted. Curiously, Dave didn't spot Herb, and if Herb spotted us, he never did say. When Herb would turn toward us, I would hide behind the man in front of me. Then I thought, Why am I doing this? I'm not misbehaving. He is! I resolved not to hide. Further, I had the strongest notion when Herb saw me to wink at him and make a gesture, forming a circle with my thumb and forefinger while the other three fingers were extended, indicating that I thought he had great taste in women as I glanced at her, then back at him. But I could not bring myself to do that. Not only that, but I broke my resolution and hid behind the man in front of me every time it appeared Herb would look in our direction.

Dave told me it was an exciting game, and wasn't it wonderful that the Bulls had won? I guess I missed a good game.

A few months later, Herb's wife phoned our house and said he was divorcing her. In another few months, about a year in all, Herb and the woman with whom I saw him at the stadium were married. I never said anything to anyone about it.

Whose Responsibility?

Having been in the school business for many years, I have noticed there seems to be a mentality that the school should be responsible for many things: reading, writing, math, sex education, values, and so on, and so forth. What makes me bristle, though, is that some people think we should be in control even when the kids are away from the school. I used to get phone calls about kids being harrassed on the way home, sometimes quite far from the school. I always talked to the kids whose names were given (sometimes no names were given!), but I always felt at a loss when things were happening away from my turf. Think of it: Have you ever heard of a parent who phoned the local movie theater or library to complain that their children were being bullied on their way home from those places? Yet school offices get many calls about this.

One incident that really blew my cork, involved one of my best friends. The boys were playing in a Little League baseball game in the middle of July at seven-thirty in the evening. Someone was shooting a BB gun at or near some of the boys playing in the game. The adults there started looking, and scared up two boys around fifteen years of age who ran from their hiding place behind a clump of bushes.

Upon learning that both boys were freshmen at Glenbard East High School, my friend, Russ Bublitz, said, "Mr. Rider better take care of those boys." Mr. Rider was the principal.

I could feel my cheeks grow hot. I bristled! I heard myself growl! Then I turned on Russ.

"Hey, Bubs, it's the middle of July; school is not in session, and even if it were, it's seven-thirty in the evening. Why is the school responsible? Don't these kids have parents?" I climbed all over him for a good five minutes. He knew he struck a nerve. He took it back a split second after he said it. "Well, may—may—maybe if he just talked to them a little," he said, trying desperately to soften his original statement.

"And why should he talk to them, Bubs? Why him? He might not even be in town, and even if he was, why? He might be on vacation somewhere." I was on a roll, and poor Bubs couldn't make me back off until I was jolly well good and ready.

"I—I—I guess it really doesn't have anything to do with him," he said.

No, it doesn't," I said emphatically. And that was that.

We are still the best of friends, and I think the guy's a prince. Let's just say I lost my cool. Whenever it comes up, and it seldom does, we have a good laugh about it.

You Haven't Changed a Bit

I am one of those people who loves attending class reunions. It brings me back to my youth, if only temporarily.

Prizes are usually given for various accomplishments, reasons and things. I'll never forget one of our reunion girls receiving a prize for having the most children—ten—at our tenth anniversary reunion!

At another, there was a prize given for the man and woman who, in the opinion of the audience, looked youngest, who had changed the least since graduation. I was one of six people nominated and, using the hand-above-the-head method (like the applause meter used on television shows years ago), yours truly was the people's choice for youngest looking among the males.

A microphone was within reach, and emboldened by the consumption of two martinis in the span of an hour, I grabbed the microphone and told my assembled classmates that I looked young from leading a virtuous life.

"I got to looking this way because of all the good, clean living I've done. Let that be a lesson to you."

The response, as expected, was "Aw sure! Sit down, P.J."

What a bunch of soreheads!

For one of our reunions, I was asked to be the master of ceremonies. I was flattered, and I accepted. I got my hands on some material appropriate for a reunion, but I don't remember the source. Here is much of the text from that little treasure:

"Consider that, at age twenty-five, we were competing for jobs and incomes. After that, it was time for spouses and kids. After that, maybe, grandchildren and vacation homes...while regarding others with envy (or glee) their waistlines, hairlines, and wrinkle lines.

"Consider that we started out before the pill. We got married first and lived together afterward. How quaint can you get?"

"Our time of youth was, in large part, before television as we know it today, before flu shots and frisbees, before frozen food, Dacron, Xerox and Grandma Moses. This was before flourescent lights, credit cards, ball point pens, and M.A.S.H. In those days, time-sharing meant togetherness, not computers. A chip meant a piece of wood, hardware meant hardware, and software wasn't even a word."

"Women rarely wore slacks. And this was before pantyhose and drip-dry clothes, before ice-makers and dishwashers, clothes dryers, freezers, electric blankets, and hairdryers, before men wore long hair and earrings."

"In our time closets were for clothes, not for coming out of, and a book about two women living together in Europe could be named 'Our Hearts Were Young and Gay.' This was before Playboy, and bunnies were small rabbits, and rabbits were not Volkswagens."

"When you were sixteen, pizza, frozen orange juice, instant coffee, and McDonald's were unheard of. You thought fast food was what you ate during Lent. You were before FM radio, stereo, tape recorders, video recorders, electric typewriters, word processors, personal computers, electronic music and disco dancing...and that's not all bad; you knew who you were dancing with, and you held onto her."

"You were before Boy George, the Beatles, and Snoopy, before vitamin pills, vodka, and the white-wine craze (whatever happened to dago-red?)"

"In your day, cigarette smoking was fashionable, grass was something we mowed, Coke was something you drank, and pot was something you cooked in. You were before day-care centers, house husbands, babysitters, computer dating, dual careers, and live-in partners.

"In your time, there were five-and-ten-cent stores where you could buy things for five and ten cents. For just a nickel or a dime you could ride the street car, make a phone call, or buy a Coke."

"You could by a new Chevy coupe for under a thousand dollars, but who could afford it then? It was a pity too, because gas was thirty cents a gallon. If anyone in those days had asked you to explain CIA, Ms., NATO, UFO, SATS, JFK, and BMW, you might have said "alphabet soup.""

"You were not before the difference between the sexes was discovered, but you were before sex change. We all made do with what we had, and ours may have been the last generation that was so dumb to think you should be married to have a baby."

"But wasn't it fun?"

My Favorite Daughter

Relax. She's my only daughter. I referred to Cindy as my favorite daughter to a group of her friends early on, and like some of those curious things, it stuck. I bring up my daughter here because she was the victim, then the happy recipient, of some very inconsistent parenting from her (favorite) dad. She had been trying every year to make the high school cheerleaders and/or the pom-poms (a group of girls who performed choreographed programs at halftime during a basketball game). One time after being cut from cheerleaders (she didn't quite make the last cut), disappointed, she decided to cut school and sulk alone at home, only to have me come home unexpectedly and become furious with her. I angrily drove her back to school in the middle of the morning and deposited her at the principal's office. Why couldn't I have been more understanding? How could I have been so blind? Who knows? At the time it seemed the right thing to do, but later I regretted having done it. But I learned from it.

A year later, she failed to heed a yield sign and demolished my prized subcompact car in the process. How frightened she was to face me! But how grateful she was when I hugged her and told her I was happy she was okay. I liked myself a lot when I did that. We can always replace a car, but we could never replace her.

About a year later, she made the pom-poms, and appeared to be quite happy. Indeed, she performed well. But in the middle of the season, she fell in love with a boy from a nearby town, and though she stayed with pom-poms, she really couldn't have cared less about it. A year later, she was enrolled at Illinois Wesleyan in Bloomington, Illinois. This had been her choice for a long time. She tried out for and became a cheerleader there. We were happy for her, since this had been denied her in high school. But after a couple of months she began to give me a sales pitch: She wanted to transfer to Elmhurst College so that she could live at home; it would be much less expensive for her "dear old dad." Translation: She wanted to be near Greg, the love of her life.

The story has a very happy ending: They were married, and have two wonderful boys.

Dave and Goliath

Some years ago our school district lost a referendum. As a result, the board of education said that many school activities were going to be dropped starting with the next school year in order to cut expenses, including all extracurricular sports at the junior high school.

My son Dave was a junior-high seventh-grader at the time. When he heard about it, he was angry and indignant. In the presence of several of his junior high school friends he loudly declared that he was going to attend the next meeting and "really tell off that board of education and make them change their minds" about dropping sports. He had participated in the intramural tackle football program as well as interscholastic basketball and track. In addition to that, he had a very good scholastic reputation (he graduated junior high school a year later with the highest scholastic grade average of all the boys, and later he was in the upper one percent of his high school, college, and medical school classes). His friends reasoned he was a good representative to talk to the board of education. A day later, Dave regretted having said it, but his friends checked in with him to make sure he'd follow through. "I think they would've killed me if I didn't," he said later.

Also, there was the problem of his father, yours truly, a principal in the district. Would he allow his son to speak against his employers for all the town to see and hear? Pretty soon I began getting phone calls from junior high-school parents: "If you've really, really got courage, you should allow your son to address the board of education."

I had decided before the phone calls began that I would allow it, even though I was uneasy about it.

127

Dave telephoned the board of education and a startled secretary asked him to hold the line while she found out whether or not a junior-high-school student would be allowed to speak at a board of education meeting. She returned and told him he had a spot on the evening's agenda.

We worked on his speech together, at his request. We softened the language of his criticism. He would respectfully implore the board of education saying that he and his classmates should not be made to suffer because of the fiscal shortcomings of the present-day caretakers.

When the night of the next board of education meeting came, Dave and I went together. He was very, very nervous. He looked at the board members who were sober-faced, unsmiling in their large leather stuffed chairs, and longed for a fire-escape or a fainting spell. Anything would be better than having to be there at that time.

The place was packed. All of Chicago's television stations were there with mini-cameras to see a little seventh-grader do battle with the big board of education. Representatives from newspapers large and small were there. This was a hot story!

When Dave's turn on the agenda came, he wisely came to the front so as to be better seen by the audience and members of the board. This position also afforded better camera angles for television. Frightened or not, this kid didn't miss a trick. He delivered his prepared speech eloquently, and at its conclusion was rewarded with the most thunderous applause he had ever heard. "It registered seven point two on the Richter Scale," he said afterward. I was very proud of him.

Later that evening we saw him on one of Chicago's network television stations. Though I had been uneasy because of my position as a principal in the district, I was happy with myself in letting him do it.

What were the lessons learned? Dave fully recognized our great society, which even allowed junior-high-school kids to speak their minds. He was also mindful of the quiet but strong support from his mother and sister. And in a private moment he told me he realized how strong I was to never waver in allowing him to give the speech in view of my vulnerable position, and how much I loved him to allow it. I was close to tears when he told me.

I received many notes and phone calls thanking me. For Dave and the entire student body, it was, perhaps one of the best civics lessons learned.

The board of education cut most sports activities as they said they would, and offered intramural basketball in place of interscholastic play. It wasn't nearly the quality of interscholastic. "It's like kissing your sister," Dave said, but he and the student body still became more sympathetic with the difficult decisions the board of education had to make, and were not the ogres they were earlier pictured to be.

The local high school was not a part of the same taxing body as the elementary school district; they were not dropping anything. The disguised blessing which came about was that the high school invited any junior-high student to attend basketball clinics during the year that interscholastic basketball was denied them at the junior high. It worked so well that they planned to continue the clinics after all extracurricular activities were reinstated at the junior high a year later.

Son of a Gun

In March of 1981 my wife, son, and I drove out to Monmouth College, a small liberal arts school with an enrollment of around eight hundred to a thousand in western Illinois. Dave was among the finalists competing for one of eleven scholarships. The best was an all-expense scholarship including tuition, room, and board. All the others were called Senate scholarships, worth two thousand per year—pretty good at that time.

I had learned a few years previously that Dave was smarter than I was, and I've been losing ground ever since. Coming from a home where both parents were educators, and blessed with a fine mind and the self-discipline to enable him to focus his concentration exclusively on an object of study, he turned out to be a star classroom performer and was in the upper one percent of his class all through school. It would take a stick of dynamite exploding under his chair to dislodge his concentration.

To be worthy of Monmouth's invitation, students had to score quite high on college entrance tests, and had to write a scholarly research paper. Dave's research had to do with checking water fountains at his high school for streptococcus germs during a one-week period of time. This turned out to be a source of embarrassment to the high school, as there were high levels of those germs in all the fountains. To the school's credit, they didn't try to suppress the information, and to Dave's credit, he didn't broadcast that dubious news scoop.

The research papers were a way to weed out over half of the contestants. However, those who were invited to the campus were not finished yet. The next step was a series of interviews for each finalist, during which a group of Monmouth faculty would question each one. It could be quite intimidating. This would conclude the competition. Parents were not allowed to accompany the prospective students for these interviews.

"Don't tell them you've been in jail," I cheerfully needled Dave as he set off for the interviews.

"Right, and I won't tell them we're here under an assumed name because of your criminal record," he teased back. We were forever needling each other with outrageous things like that. Elaine, my wife, went to a coffee clatch the school had arranged for moms. The dads were invited to the student union for coffee and to watch the college NCAA basketball finals on television.

When Dave finished the interviews and returned to my side, we watched the games for a while. The conversation eventually turned to the interviews. He was asked many questions, some of the answers of which I was sure were designed to count toward winning or losing a scholarship. Here's an example: You are the star pitcher and you need nine more scoreless innings to break a conference record. You're leading five-to-nothing in the ninth inning, two out, and a runner on second. One more out and you make history. The hitter singles to left field. The play at the plate will be close, and could go either way. You are the cut-off man in this situation. What do you do?

"What'd you answer?" I asked.

"I cut off the throw and nailed the batter at second. It's the wisest thing to do, if you're a team player. We've won the game, and though I don't break the record for scoreless innings, it's an unselfish play. I'm sure they liked my answer," he said. I liked his answer as well.

"What else did they ask?"

"One question was, 'Who in the world, living or dead, do you most admire, and why?'"

Some images came immediately to me: Winston Churchill

who rallied his people from the brink of disaster; Lincoln who had to make heart-wrenching decisions; Ghandi; Eisenhower...

Dave answered very casually, somewhat like the late Richard Burton when he threw away a line," I told them it was you, Dad, no question about it. You taught me how to study, hit a baseball, play basketball, and just about everything. You were a model of honesty and integrity. I meant it sincerely."

I'm sure Dave didn't mean to blow me away, but it took me by complete surprise. I was stunned and found I was unable to speak for a few moments. It took my breath away. I believe I began to say something appreciative, but it came out sounding more like a temporary stutter. I felt my eyes get cloudy and, yes, I felt a tear roll down my face. The only way I could keep from breaking down completely was to hug him. He understood, and hugged me back until I regained my composure. To this day, that little scene remains one of the big moments in my life.

Dave came in second in the competition and was awarded a Senate scholarship and the boy who won the all-expense scholarship turned out to be his best friend, and his best man at his wedding a few years later.

The Prayer Shot

During my son Dave's senior-high-school year, his team had a basketball game scheduled at Libertyville, one of the far northern suburbs. Near the end of the first half, with ten seconds left, the ball bounced off a Libertyville player and went out of bounds. Our team, Glenbard East, took a time out and discussed briefly how we were going to get another basket before halftime. Because Mike Biegielski, a strapping six-foot-five boy, had a hot hand (fourteen points thus far), the coach directed the inbound pass (near half-court) to go to Dave, who, in turn, was instructed to look for Mike along the baseline. When the ball was inbounded to him, it seemed to Dave that the entire Libertyville student body was guarding Mike. Clearly, he wasn't open. Meanwhile, the seconds were ticking away: five seconds, four, three....He did the only thing he could in these circumstances being about forty feet from the basket near half-court; he took the jumper from there, and it went in, hitting nothing but the net. It was clearly a lucky shot, what is sometimes referred to as a "prayer shot." Then the half ended. A roar went out from the Glenbard fans, a loud groan from the hometown Libertyville rooters. On their way to the locker room, our kids had to pass in front of a large crowd of the home team fans, and they were not kind, shouting obscenities and other things: "Hey number ten, what a lucky shot," and the like.

The next September, I drove Dave and his belongings to Monmouth College. When we arrived, there were several new college kids like Dave moving in with their stuff. Since most were freshmen, they began introducing themselves to one another: "I'm Mike Lowery from Naperville," "John Sullivan from Freeport," and so forth. I was more of an observer on the edge.

Two of the boys were from Libertyville, and I could see they were looking at Dave as if they had seen him before. Finally one of them asked him, "Did you play basketball at Lombard High School?"

"Yes, I did, for Glenbard East," Dave replied.

"Were you number ten?"

Dave nodded, knowing what was coming next.

"What kind of a lucky shot was that just before halftime," he asked, laughing now.

Dave had been through this before with his own friends at East. "Whaddaya mean, lucky shot? I figured the wind," he said, licking and sticking out an index finger, "times the circumference of the ball, plus the degree of the arch. You think that was easy?"

This revelation was met by loud laughter. They were friends now, enjoying each other's company. Such are the curious twists of fate.

God's Cruel Trick On Golfers

I'm into golf these days. I didn't play a lick until recently, about a year ago. I think I'm hooked. I really don't play well, and I don't know if I ever will. I'm the kind of erratic player who might tee off and hit the ball over the green, or I might par a hole, but it's sandwiched between an eight before and a seven after. It is, indeed, a humbling game. I understood how humbling it can be when I watched Jack Nicklaus on television, one of the greatest golfers to play the game, get stuck in a sand trap, after which it took him ten strokes to get out and onto the green. Disgusted with himself, he heaved his pitching wedge over the green from the sand trap. I'm sure most golfers were sympathetic with him about what had happened that day.

One day, at a principals' seminar, Bill Glasser, a psychiatrist who's big in education and has written books like Schools Without Failure and Reality Therapy, told this story:

"God plays a cruel trick on golfers. You're out there trying to do your best, but accomplishing very little. You're slicing on your drives; you're dubbing your fairway shots, each going only twenty feet or so; you're missing easy putts, and chipping shots into the lake. The one or two shots you do manage to shoot straight go directly into the sand trap anyway. Just about the time you're licked, defeated, and ready to throw your clubs, bag and all, into one of the deeper lakes, God grants you one good shot, and the whole thing starts all over again."

I know what he means.

About the Author

A Chicagoan by birth, a Floridian by choice, Joseph Alengo has lived most of his life in the Chicago area, attending schools in Chicago and becoming interested in guiding youth in the process.

As a varsity basketball starter in high school and a player in junior college, he had fun, but didn't particularly distinguish himself.

After a two-year hitch in the U.S. Navy and teaching high school speech and English, he and his wife and two children settled in Lombard, Illinois, a western Chicago suburb, where Joseph spent most of his education career serving in several capacities: teaching junior-high language arts, social studies, and physical education, and coaching boys' and girls' interscholastic basketball teams, as well as handling the "Little Theater" sponsorship.

After achieving a measure of success in Lombard, Joseph was assigned to an elementary school as a sixth-grade teacher and as the boys' and girls' coach for flag football and basketball. "I started in high school and worked my way down," he says. In reality, he was being groomed for the position of principal a few years later.

Somewhere along the way Joseph became a radio disc jockey for local radio station WKDC, Elmhurst, playing his beloved jazz and swing ("Last on your dial, but first in your heart"). He calls the experience "the best job I ever had—playing my favorite music and being paid for it."

Joseph currently resides in North Fort Myers with his wife, and has added playing golf to his list of favorite things to do.